CONUNDRUM

D1566521

CONUNDRUM

By Susan Cory

ACKNOWLEDGMENTS

The characters in Conundrum bear no resemblance to my classmates and professors at Harvard's Graduate School of Design. Would you really want to read a story about a bunch of nice architects?

I am grateful to many people for their help in wrestling this story down onto the page /screen. For virtual hand-holding as I crossed over from the visual world into the verbal one I'd like to thank my fellow writers at Sisters-in-Crime, especially the Guppies.

Heartfelt thanks and admiration go to Anne Wagner, Pam Simpson, and Kat Lancaster for their editing expertise. For helping me to plug plot holes I'm indebted to Eve Spangler and Martha Craumer.

A special thanks goes to Narween Otto, my critique partner, for her sensitive ear to dialogue, and to S.J. Rozan for her talent as a teacher equal to hers as a crime fiction writer.

For technical help, I'm grateful to Katie Hallett for her psychological insights, Alex Harpp for her legal take on Norman's tape, and Detective Danny Marshall of Cambridge Major Crimes for his explanation of the jurisdictional chain of command as well as a tour of the new Cambridge Police HQ.

My husband, Dan Tenney, deserves a medal for patiently reading through every latest installment dished out at dinnertime and for giving me his feedback diplomatically.

Finally, this book would never have been started without the encouragement of my friends and fellow architects Gail Lindsey and Olga Vysatova McCord. I so wish you both were here to see it in print. I dedicate *Conundrum* to you.

"Nothing stands out so conspicuously,
or remains so firmly fixed in the memory,
as something which you have blundered."

—*Marcus Tullius Cicero*

CHAPTER 1

Iris Reid loved Monday mornings when she had a house in construction. She couldn't wait to get back to the building site to check on its progress. Her old jeep bumped up the rutted dirt driveway in the upscale Boston suburb of Lincoln. Dirty patches of snow pock-marked the ground and Iris could see her breath condensing on the windshield. After maneuvering around a sharp turn her eyes lit up—the three-level skeleton of the house faced her. It stepped gracefully up and into the hillside, with bright blue tarps over its flat roofs snapping in the wind. Several balconies, cantilevered in a cubist configuration, now sprouted from the volumes of the main house. She cut the engine and studied her Modernist creation, savoring the changes since last week's visit.

Then she spotted Frank's Dodge pickup. Damn. That was the only drawback to construction—having to deal with contractors. This one rated about a 7 on the 1-to-10 misogyny scale. It seemed to bug Frank more that she had gone to Harvard than that she was female or an architect. He'd learned this fact from her website and now made a point of calling her "Hey, Harvard." Still, the house was coming together.

For this design, Iris had used an arsenal of 'green' features. From the insulating sod roof to the wood floors reclaimed from a Vermont barn, this house had impeccable environmental 'cred' and she was hoping to get it certified as LEED platinum. But its piece de resistance—the Meeker geo-thermal energy system—had been contributed by her client.

Years earlier, her former classmate, Norman Meeker (or more likely one of his underlings) had designed a system of running water pipes 150 feet underground, harnessing the earth's core temperature of 52 degrees to modulate heating and cooling. It was simple, brilliant and had made Norman's fortune. His first fortune, that is. By now he had three or four major patents on clever energy-saving building products. He'd used his architecture school training in a far more lucrative way than the rest of them. Even in school, Norman had affected the avuncular manner of one whose success would out-pace his peers'. This manner had always irritated Iris, so when he'd called her a year earlier to discuss her designing a house for him, she'd been ambivalent. But she'd always said a plum project and steep fee could give her the patience of a saint. Now she was getting a chance to test this.

Iris climbed the building frame to the top level, the main living section of the open floor plan. The roof tarp cast an eerie blue glow over the space. Frank, talking on his cell phone, scowled at her, then flipped the phone shut. He sauntered over, jaw at the lead, his tool-belt swinging low on his hips like an outlaw's holster. "Hey, Harvard, the windows for the living room aren't gonna fit."

She groaned inwardly. Iris had created a composition with the windows and doors that allowed little margin for error. Casements, stationaries, transoms, French doors—all fit together like a Chinese puzzle. Contractors hated not having room to fudge, so Frank had been predicting disaster from the moment he had first read the drawings and specs. Now he looked smug.

"Okaaaay, let's go over this," she said. "Where's the problem?"

"Marvin dropped off the windows late Friday. We uncrated them and laid them out like you drew, and the whole thing is 1/2" too wide. It won't fit." Frank made a dismissive sweep toward the windows. Iris registered the abrupt silencing of power tools as several carpenters stopped to watch the show. "When they ganged the two doors and stationary window, they made it wider than you put on the drawings. I told you it was too tight to work. Now my schedule's gonna be shot to hell."

Iris headed stiffly over to where the windows and doors had been laid out on the plywood sub-floor amidst the muddy imprints of lug soles. She pulled out a tape to take her own measurements as Frank glowered above her, hands on hips.

She brushed past him to consult her drawings set out on a makeshift table. There had to be some solution other than ordering a narrower window. She squinted at the critical string of dimensions, blurred by coffee rings. Then she leaned back. Thank god I've picked up some tricks over the years. She called out to Frank, "Keep your shirt on. I made the door frames triple-studded to allow for something like this. We can swap out one of those studs on the latch side with a one-by, and that'll give you your extra half-inch plus."

She noted his disappointed look. The other carpenters turned back to their work smirking. She shook her head. She hated the head-butting that often went with her job. They should teach child psychology in architecture school. It would be more useful than some of the esoteric theory courses she had dozed through.

"Measure all the rest of the windows to see if we need any more adjustments," she shouted over the roar as the compressor came back on.

"I may have to put in a change order," he yelled.

"Yeah, yeah... you do that. Oh, and Frank... don't forget that the June 4th deadline is drop-dead. You've got three months. Norman's planning to have an important dinner party here that night, so delays aren't an option."

"Tell that to the Poggenpohl kitchen people," he called after her as she headed for the temp stairs before he could come up with any more complaints. Most contractors, by this point in the job, realized that the house was looking good and started respecting her judgment. Or at least they'd let up on baiting her. For whatever reasons, Frank didn't get it.

She climbed down two levels to her destination—the wine cellar. A rough-walled cave with a barrel-vaulted ceiling had been carved out of a stone section of the hill. This would become a hidden room, accessed by pressing the right spot on the outer room's paneling.

She took out a clipboard and jotted down dimensions for ordering the shelving, wine refrigerator, and table that Norman had requested. He knew very little about wine but wanted a state-of-the-art wine cellar. Ever since his wife had left him, he had been positioning himself as a "player" in the Boston middle-aged dating circuit. For a guy with a Calligula hairdo with one inch bangs, who walked toes-out like a duck, this was an uphill battle. Every possible electronic device had to be put on a remote control, 007 style. With his status as a "green" activist in business, his Toyota Prius was a given, but he had also purchased a sleek, black 1995 Porsche 928—his one toy that had Iris salivating. She had offered to take the Porsche as her architectural fee.

"We belong in that car, Sheba, not Norman," she'd lamented to her dog.

When it came to the wine cellar, Iris was on home turf. Her father had given her tutorials on vintages, varietals, and their proper care. By now she was a true connoisseur, able to create the perfect wine *cave*. The idea of a dork like Norman using it as a backdrop for a seduction attempt struck her as a crime.

CHAPTER 2

Later that morning Iris worked on a freehand sketch in the turreted home office of her Victorian house. She was hunched over the section of a table she'd designed that tipped up to form a drafting board. The loud "thunk" that announced something heavy coming through the mail slot nearby barely registered. But when Sheba, her six-year-old basset hound, waddled to the front vestibule, the clicking of her toenails on the wood floor roused Iris. She collected the mail, placing some bills in Sheba's mouth for transport to the kitchen floor. The dog loved this "job". Iris muttered about the latest misspellings of her four-letter, Anglo-Saxon surname, R-E-I-D— those fourth grade teachers with their 'i before e except after c' drill had a lot to answer for. Tossing aside the inevitable flyers and catalogs, she came to a book wrapped in plastic: *Twentieth Reunion of Harvard's Graduate School of Design—Class of 1988* and stood transfixed, staring at the cover.

It wasn't a surprise. After all, Norman was the reunion's chairman. He had been nattering on about it for weeks. It was due to the small, highly selective opening-night dinner in three month's time that they were racing to finish the house. Norman was determined to show it off to one of their former classmates, C.C. Okuyama, who was now editing a big-time architectural magazine.

Iris was braced for it. Still, her insides felt knotted.

She headed mechanically to her kitchen window seat, and opened the directory with one finger as if it were radioactive, searching for five particular names. Then she speed-dialed her best friend Ellie.

"Have you seen it yet?"

"What?"

"The reunion book. It's in today's mail."

"Call you back." Ellie lived around the corner in Iris' Cambridge neighborhood.

Fifteen minutes later Ellie tapped on the kitchen window. She hung her parka on a hook in the mudroom alcove, then followed Iris back to the kitchen window seat, where Sheba jumped up to nestle between them. "It looks like all 5 of them plan to come," Ellie began. "You know what that means."

"They didn't come to the tenth or fifteenth. Why now? Why all of them?" Iris rested a fingernail between two teeth, then quickly removed it. "Are we really going to do this?"

"We could head out of town for the weekend to avoid running into them—just let it blow over."

YES! Iris thought. Let's go up to that spa in Vermont and take long walks with Sheba, and get massages, and when we come back they'll be gone. "Well, if you don't want to go..."

"Then again, C.C.'s going to be there. Norman's house would be perfect for her magazine and the publicity would be great for you. Something good could come out of this. Besides, we always said that if we could just get all five of them in one room again..."

"I know, but it's completely hopeless. How can we possibly find out who followed Carey onto that balcony twenty years ago?"

"If we can steer the conversation that way, we might be able to piece together people's whereabouts at the party. We've talked about this."

Iris felt the invasion of cold seeping through the window glass. Outside, the wind was rustling the dead leaves in her garden.

"Besides, the attempt alone might stop your nightmares. Have you been sleeping at all? I'm worried about you."

Iris knew that the gray shadows under her eyes had returned. "It's this reunion business that's started them up again. This happens every five years, remember? They'll recede on their own after it's over."

"Darlin', it's been twenty years. You've got to let go. It wasn't your job to protect Carey."

"Tell that to him. Tell him to stop haunting me."

"You sound like you're in a horror movie. Aren't we being a wee bit over-dramatic?"

"He's not going to leave me alone until I find his murderer."

"Oh, come on. You told the police what you suspected and they wouldn't believe you. What more are you supposed to do? Maybe we should stage an exorcism. Have you been biting your nails?"

"No." She tucked her hands under the table.

"Norman's welcome letter says G.B.'s going to be there too. You know, I've been wondering if we should add him to the suspect list. The graduation party *was* at his apartment."

"Why would he kill Carey? G.B. wasn't one of the jealous classmates."

"He might have had an affair with him. Maybe Carey was going to expose him for sleeping with students. G.B. wouldn't have wanted to lose his Harvard teaching gig."

"Maybe. That would bring it to six suspects." She stared at her ragged cuticles, blinking. "All I know is that Carey didn't fall off that balcony. And it was one of these six, I'd stake my life on it, who drugged him, shoved him to his death—and got away with murder."

CHAPTER 3

Right after Ellie left, the phone in Iris' office rang. She ran from the kitchen to the next room to answer "Reid Associates" in her faux-receptionist voice.

"Iris, it's C.C.— C.C. Okuyama from GSD. Long time, yadda, yadda… I'm calling because I understand from G.B. that you've designed a house for Norman that I might want to put in cuttingedgedecor. I'm not making any promises, but we're doing a "green" issue and my managing editor says that I need to dig up some examples outside the New York area for a change. But it's always murder to find anything decent in the provinces."

Iris could picture C.C. rolling her eyes and running her stubby fingers through her black page-boy. Sheba appeared at Iris' knee, favorite hide-a-squirrel toy in her mouth, making low, growly noises. For some reason the phone ringing triggered a "play" button in her head. Iris glared down at her and mouthed "no!"

"Great, C.C. I'd be happy to show you the house. We've used several of Norman's inventions and we're going through accreditation for LEED platinum. When do you want to see it?

"G.B. roped me into that Friday night reunion shindig Norman's hosting, so why don't you show me around then?"

Sheba pulled one of the baby squirrels out of its tree trunk and pranced around with it, trying to get her mistress' attention. Iris swivelled away from her.

"Actually, I haven't decided yet if I'm going to the reunion. But I can give you a private tour that week-end."

"No, no, I'm not sure how long I'll be staying up there. It's more convenient for me if you show me the house while I'm also doing the dinner thing. Two birds, one stone. By the way, Iris, I looked at your website. You only have a few published write-ups listed. How about showing a little Harvard hustle? You should jump at opportunities like this. So, shall I assume that I'll see you in three months at the Friday night dinner?

Iris massaged her temples. Sheba dropped to the floor with a dramatic sigh, her paw stuck in the tree trunk.

"Fine. I'll be there."

"Oh, and Iris, don't mention this possible feature to Norman, okay?" Click.

Iris turned to look down at her dog. "You squeeze oranges, Sheba, you get orange juice. These people never change." Sheba gave her an "I'm ignoring you too" look.

She'd call Ellie to let her know that, apparently, she was going to at least the Friday night portion of the reunion. Maybe she would get lucky and someone would talk about that long-ago graduation party. As C.C. had put it: "two birds, one stone."

CHAPTER 4

In early June, 1988, Iris Reid was making a long, careful slice with an x-acto knife. The earlier manic energy in the large open fishbowl of GSD's architecture studio had settled into a workmanlike hum. Snatches of Bob Marley leaked from behind a walled-in desk to her right, warring with Jimi Hendrix coming from the left. Harder to tune out was the pungent stench of pepperoni pizza, cigarette butts and unwashed students.

The sheet of white foam-core under her knife started to go blurry. Two in the morning was an inadvisable time for model-building—especially at the tail end of a triple all-nighter. She needed another infusion of vending machine coffee. She hesitated, running her tongue over her teeth. They already felt fuzzy.

A crown of auburn curls moved across the top of her wall, followed by the rest of Ellie leaning into the opening of her enclosure. "Let the slaves rise up and slay their oppressor. Let my people go."

"You can leave anytime, you know, Moses." Iris said. "There's a soft pillow waiting for you two blocks away."

"Ha! You just want me to show up tomorrow with an unfinished model like yours. And you already have a job offer, so this crit doesn't even matter for you." Ellie crouched down to study Iris' building. "I predict three more hours to finish it, darlin'. That means two hours of sleep max and another presentation with filthy hair."

"It's my signature look. And you, Ms. Gardenia-smell, what's the status of your model?"

"Actually, I'm done. I came by to gloat on my way home. I'll be thinking of you as I drift off to sleep. Ta, ta."

"Why has it taken me three years to recognize your mean streak?" she called to Ellie's retreating back. Iris turned back to her work in despair. Why had she changed her floor plan last week? Would it really be so bad if it wasn't done? It looked okay the way it was. She'd rest her head on her arms. Just for a few minutes…

"Aaaaagh!" an ear-splitting scream rang through the open studio.

Iris shook herself awake and raised herself up to peer out above her wall. Classmates were running toward the commotion several cubicles away.

Carey, the class superstar, whose voice never rose above a raspy whisper, was staring wild-eyed at his cardboard model. "Who did this?" he screamed, his waving arms still holding a bottle of lemonade from the nearby vending machines.

The circle of students gaped first at him, shocked that he was capable of shouting, then down at the large, brown coffee stain bleeding over a village that Carey had spent the last week constructing. Even some of the tiny trees had coffee dripping from their branches.

"What happened?"

"Someone spilled coffee on Carey's model. Do you believe it?" got whispered through the crowd.

Iris waited for a sleep-deprived classmate to mumble an embarrassed apology while Carey began pacing his cubicle like a caged lion, wordlessly jabbing his finger toward the model as if he were conducting a silent argument. His face was becoming splotchy with suppressed rage and Iris worried that his brain might start to bubble.

She couldn't take her eyes off him. For three years this guy had been like her younger brother. She had helped him find his classrooms first year. She'd reminded him of his upcoming exams. She had even tried to diffuse the growing swirl of jealousy around him by pointing out his obliviousness to his own talent. In all that time, Carey had never shown any emotion but enthusiasm or his default dreamy half-smile. Certainly never rage.

"Isn't someone going to at least admit they did it?" Iris appealed to the heads lined up along Carey's wall.

"This really sucks," someone volunteered.

"Yeah, sorry, man."

"I didn't see anyone, did you?"

Heads shook, shoulders shrugged, then people drifted away to finish their own projects, relieved that this hadn't happened to them.

Iris grabbed a roll of paper towels from a nearby desk and started dabbing at the stains. She knew there was nothing to be salvaged, and the final critique was the next day—that day actually. Displaying their models and pinning up their boards to be analyzed would be the culmination of three years of total immersion. Well-known architects had already flown in from New York and Berlin to be on their studio's jury. This time, there was no way that Carey could dazzle them with his presentation.

The two of them stood looking down at the site of destruction. A luxo lamp aimed in close on the model released the acrid smell of scorched coffee. Arms wrapped around his skinny chest, rocking back and forth, Carey emitted a long visceral moan. Iris wanted to put a reassuring arm around his shoulder, but knew he didn't like to be touched. A stillness came over him, followed by a subtle shift in his stance, a straightening. Iris watched him look around his cubicle as if returning from a trance. He moved to his second desk and stared for a minute. Then he began to roll up his drawings, shove them into his backpack, and dejectedly slide it onto a shoulder. He looked up at her. "I'm going home now, Iris. Thanks for trying to help me."

"Good idea. Get some rest," she said, unable to think of any encouraging words.

Iris watched him grab his ruined model and trudge away.

She couldn't help wondering who would do such a mean thing.

***

Three days later, at their graduation party, Iris congratulated Carey on the triumph of his final crit. "You had those critics eating out of your hand. When you started talking about those glass roof tiles I thought that they were going to offer you a job on the spot."

Carey looked at his feet. "One of them did. But you really saved me, Iris, when you came over in the middle of the night with that spray paint. I'd thought that my model was a goner."

Iris smiled at the memory of her brainstorm. "I had a can left over from painting a chair I'd found put out on the street. Sorry about waking you up."

"Did it look okay? The trees were a little gloppy."

"It looked perfect. Everyone was blown away."

"Your crit went well too. I love how sculptural your designs always are. And making all the walls either stone or glass was pure poetry." Carey stared around at the large loft. The high-ceilinged space had a streamlined kitchen open to a living room with floor-to-ceiling bookshelves along one side." Whose place is this? Oh, yeah, G.B.'s. It's really cool."

Gilles Broussard had started teaching three years before, in tandem with their class starting the Master of Architecture program. For that reason, or perhaps due to the high percentage of cute young men on the roster, he had become sentimentally attached to their class. He enjoyed swanning around the design studio, well-tailored jacket draped over a shoulder, stinking Gauloise stuck between thumb and middle finger, complaining—"Where are the new ideas?" Students prayed that he wouldn't make this comment while staring at their slaved-over project.

"So, you've never been here before either?" Iris asked.

Carey looked confused. "You mean students get invited here?"

Iris could have kicked herself. She hadn't meant to underscore that Carey hadn't been in the inner circle of overly ambitious, catty students who had clustered around G.B. Her boyfriend, Will, had been in that group. He had often been invited over with his roommate, Adam. The two of them made a photogenic pair—Will Reynolds with his pierced ear and hip charm and Adam Lincoln with the clean, chiseled looks of an astronaut.

"I think so. At least Will said he'd been here before." It had seemed uncool for Iris to ask Will what had gone on here. Her relationship with him had blazed along, on-and-off during third year, until Iris' vague sense of distrust wore away the connection. They had broken up the week before, when gearing up for their final reviews and Iris still hadn't had a chance to process it. Now she searched the room for him.

"He's over there by the windows," Carey said, reading her mind. They both spotted Will, who must have been telling an amusing story. The group around him were laughing. Iris shivered, then wondered why Carey, whom the inner circle despised for showing them up, always seemed so fascinated with their members.

"Hey, Iris, there you are!" Ellie elbowed her way through the crowd. She tipped her head towards the tall, friendly-looking man following close behind her. "You remember Mack, don't you?" Carey drifted off like fog.

Of course Iris remembered Mack. She was thrilled that her best friend had found such a nice guy. Ellie had met him, a med school student, in the laundry room of their apartment building. They hugged in greeting.

Ellie gave her a once-over and whistled. "I didn't know you owned a dress. Why haven't I seen this before?"

"It took three years of forgetting to eat to fit in it again. It's from high school. Getting a chance to finally shower made me feel like dressing up." Iris knew that the short, tight dress showed off her long legs, and the neckline displayed a tease of cleavage. The green color intensified her hazel eyes. She even had mascara on. Her almost-black hair was piled in a loose, sexy chignon. She wanted Will to have this final impression of her burned into his memory-bank when they went their separate ways.

"So, Iris, has it sunk in yet that you're done with boot camp? Ellie seems to be in shock still." Mack sent Ellie an affectionate look.

"We're done?" Iris said in mock-surprise. "We never have to go back to the studio? YES!" she shrieked, pumping her fist in the air. A few people looked over and grinned.

"We've stopped in to say good-bye to a few people on our way to the Turtle Café for dinner. Want to join us?" Ellie asked.

Iris did want to, but said "No, you guys go. I've got to get home to finish packing. My train leaves for New York first thing in the morning."

Ellie grabbed her hands. "Now, you've promised me, girl, that you won't disappear into your new life in the big city. New York is only a few hours from here."

"Are you kidding? We've been watching each other's backs for so long, I won't be able to function without you. I'll probably have to come back every weekend. You'll be begging me to stay away." Iris bent down as the two friends folded each other in their arms.

After they left, Iris wandered over to the kitchen island to pour herself a Coke. She wanted wine, but needed the caffeine to stay awake to pack. As she drank, she peered over at the bookshelves in the living room. Seriously? She crossed the space. Pulling a book out, she confirmed that it had been dust-jacketed in white vellum. Every single book had gotten this treatment. You couldn't tell a book's title until you opened it to inspect the real jacket below. Now here was an example of form over function. And it belonged to a professor training her in her profession?

She made a sweep of the room, looking for Carey. She wanted to say a final farewell, but before she could spot him she got caught in the headlights of a look from Alyssa, the class Queen Bee. Iris steeled herself as Alyssa strode over, cashmere cardigan knotted just-so around her neck. Even atop high heels, Alyssa barely reached five feet, but in her mind, she commanded attention.

"A little bird tells me that you and Will have finally broken up."

Iris winced at Alyssa's little-girl voice, then at her words.

"You've got to stop talking to birds, Alyssa," was her only response. Given Iris' eight-inch height advantage, it was easy for her to see over Alyssa's head, as she willed the busybody to go away. She saw G.B. huddled in a corner in deep discussion with one of his acolytes.

As Alyssa's voice chirped on, Iris saw a tableau over by the living area's exposed brick wall. Carey had moved to the refreshment table and Will was offering him a plate of brownies. Bizarrely, her mind flashed on an image of the witch from Hansel and Gretel offering sweets to the children. Or maybe Carey resembled an eager puppy more than Hansel.

But when Iris caught the words "would have sewn his zipper shut at the beginning of the year," her attention snapped back to Alyssa.

"What did you say?"

"I said it's about time you broke up with Will. His affair with Sharon Abramson must have been tough to ignore." Alyssa casually poured herself a plastic cup of Almaden chablis from a green glass jug.

Iris felt an impact, as if she'd been kicked in the stomach. She leaned against the island counter. So her feeling had been right. Will had been cheating on her. What kind of guy is that lacking in a sense of decency? What a scum-bag! Alyssa was studying her. Iris conjured up a bored mask and tossed off "Thank god he's not my problem anymore. Now I've really got to go pack for my train to New York."

She grabbed her purse and said over her shoulder "exuse me, Alyssa," as she aimed toward the fire stairs. Her self-control wasn't going to hold out long enough to wait for the elevator to rise to the seventh floor. The sound in the space seemed to crescendo into a cacophony of laughing shrieking voices, but got chopped off when the fire door swung closed behind her. She felt the heat rising in her cheeks as she crumpled down onto the landing, letting tears flow until her eyes stung.

After the time it took to catalog all of Will's suspicious late-night absences and to progress from despair to anger to resignation, she wiped her eyes and plodded down the remaining flights to the exit door. Out on the sidewalk, she blinked in the hazy afternoon glare, disoriented until a startled cry pierced the suffocating stillness. Lifting her head, she saw a blur. What was that? It was huge. It looked like it flew off the balcony on the top floor—a dark silhouette against the sunlit brick. She shielded her eyes. Oh, my God—it was a person! It was falling straight toward her, but she couldn't move. She began to hyperventilate, her eyes were riveted on the torpedo hurtling at her. It was going to land on top of her. Oh, no! Not him! She recognized Carey right above her—arms outstretched as if flying, eyes wide as if startled, mouth open as if caught in a scream. His body thudded on the sidewalk before her, an empty, hollow sound. She stared down in mute horror, watching as the rivulets of her friend's blood pooled around her sandals.

CHAPTER 5

This was ridiculous, Iris thought. She had the concentration of a gnat. Positioned at her favorite window table at the Paradise Café, the one with the view of frustrated drivers backed up at the Porter Square traffic light, she had read and reread the same paragraph in her Architectural Record for the last 20 minutes. It was early May, the tail end of New England's mud season, and the café's heavy wood door was propped open to allow the earthy spring air to waft in.

She glanced over one more time at the subject of her distraction: Luc, the café's owner and chef who was perched on a stool behind a long, mahogany coffee counter. He was tapping on an i-Pad as his barista, a guy with a goatee whose name Iris couldn't remember, worked the espresso machine. The cheerful space was humming with the post-nine-a.m. crowd of the self-employed. Iris inhaled the aroma of strong coffee mingled with the smell of freshly baked pastries.

How old did Ellie say she thought he was? Mid-thirties? Iris herself was forty-four but still managed to draw appreciative looks from men. She'd never seen a girlfriend hovering around Luc in the four months since he'd opened the place. Then again, she and Ellie had never been here for lunch or dinner. Mornings were when they used the café to transition from private life to work life in their home offices.

Luc was wearing a thick, black, ribbed sweater with a zipper that angled diagonally down from his Adam's apple about nine inches. She was fascinated with that zipper and its asymmetry. With his head bowed, she could also study the different yellows in his hair—from pale pinot grigio to deep, buttery chardonnay. He had it scraped back into a ponytail that was looped around like a snail.

Maybe she could buddy up to Louise, the waitress with the stud in her nose. Louise might know if Luc was involved with someone. Iris watched his lips form private little smiles which appeared and disappeared. He was adorable. What was she thinking? Of course he had a girlfriend. Why hadn't she paid him more attention when he'd drop by her table from time to time? But then again, if they ever did get into a relationship and it crashed and burned, as most of hers did, she and Ellie would be out of a perfect breakfast spot. Ellie would be pissed. Was it worth the risk? She sighed and swept her magazine into her tote, giving him a final regretful look just as his head rose to scan the room and he noticed her gaze.

She busied herself refolding the *Boston Globe,* returning it to the basket by the door and slipping on her black leather jacket.

"Are you leaving already?" Luc had materialized at her table. "I was finishing writing up the menu for tonight and wanted to join you. You looked so sad just now."

He sat down and she sank back into the seat facing him. "Oh, no—I was just thinking… about something. I guess I could loiter a bit longer." She pulled her eyes away from the zipper. "Do you mind if I ask you a personal question?"

Luc looked slightly alarmed. "Okay."

"How come you don't wear clogs? I thought all chefs were required to wear them? Isn't it in a contract somewhere?"

He let out a deep laugh. He had a wonderful laugh. "I hate clogs. They're so ugly. Chefs wear them because they're comfortable when you're on your feet all day." He displayed a foot shod in supple, brown calfskin. "I had these boots made in Italy, and they give me much more support than clogs. Besides, one of the perks of owning this place is that I get to set the dress code. Gee, is that the most personal thing you want to know about me? I'm crushed."

She started to blush. "You can ask me something now if you want. Fair's fair."

He looked down at her left hand. She thought he was going to ask about the man's watch she always wore, but instead, with a finger, he traced over a one inch scar near her thumb.

"How'd you get this?"

She looked down too. "Ah, that's an architect's tattoo. We all have them. It's from an x-acto knife slicing me instead of the cardboard model I was working on in school. If you don't have at least one hand scar, you're not a real architect. Don't chefs have knife scars?" She reached for his hands to look.

"If they do, it means that their knife skills seriously suck." He displayed his unmarked hands with their long, elegant fingers, pinning her with his blue eyes—the quiet blue-gray kind, not the intense shade that jumped out at you. She liked that his nose was wide at the bridge, saving him from being conventionally handsome. It roughened his edges a bit.

"The other day when I stopped by your table, you and Ellie were talking about a class reunion. Did you guys decide to go?"

"So far we're only signed up for the Friday night dinner. It's being held at a house that I designed for the reunion chairman."

"That's right—you're an architect and Ellie writes books about architects. Who's this client?"

"A guy from our class, Norman Meeker, who went into business instead of architecture."

"Isn't he that billionaire who invented all those eco building products?"

"That's him. I forget how famous he is now; I just think of him as my irritating client. Last year he hired me to build him a trophy house to show off his inventions."

As she talked about Norman an inspiration struck her. "As the reunion chairman, he asked me to find a good caterer for the opening night party. Does the

Paradise do that?" Actually she had been in talks for a week with two catering firms neither of which were being particularly accommodating.

"That's a co-incidence. I've been planning to start up a catering side business. I hadn't gotten around to advertising it yet. I did a lot of that from my restaurant in Rome before I moved back here."

"You had your own restaurant in Rome? You seem too young for that."

"It was a small place that I had with a partner, but I ended up working all the time. I'm trying to pace myself better here."

"Then are you sure you want to get into catering? Won't that take up a lot of time along with the restaurant?"

"It's a question of economics. I have a second chef coming over from Italy soon to help out in the kitchen. I need to keep expanding." Luc glanced over toward the coffee counter to make sure that goatee-guy had the trickle of customers under control. Most of the crowd were contentedly nursing lattes while pecking on their laptops.

"The dinner is in a month, on Friday June 4th. Would that work for you? It's only for 10 people because GSD reunions split up into third-year design studios for the first night. Should I tell Norman that I've secured a caterer? Oh, hang on. Maybe I should warn you about these people first. Have you read *'Lord of the Flies'*? 'Eat or be eaten' could be their mantra. You should be out of the direct line of fire, but there could be collateral damage."

"I only care whether Norman pays his bills. In the restaurant business you have to learn to deal with entitled types. But it sounds like *you* may need a bodyguard."

"Are you volunteering?" She decided not to mention her own brown belt in karate, however rusty it was.

"Sure. I could decapitate anyone who got out of line with the canape tray. I play a mean game of ultimate frisbee."

"Excellent. There will be several heads at the table I'd like to see on a platter."

Luc grinned, then yawned and shook his head. "Sorry, I was at the market at six this morning. I'm going home to crash for a few hours. Let's talk later about the catering." In one fluid movement, he was up and out the door.

CHAPTER 6

Iris marched up the hill to Ellie's house, half a block away, and plopped down at the kitchen table. "I thought we were flirting, but then he turned a switch and vanished. He was probably just being friendly and I scared him off. I'm such a fool." She grimaced at a nail bitten down to the quick.

"Are you done? Tell me when you're done, darlin'." Ellie made a show of starting to empty her dishwasher.

Iris sat for a few minutes in silence. "Fine, I'm done. Now you can tell me what an idiot I am."

Ellie put away some dishes and turned to her. "You're not an idiot, at least not for that. I think you and Luc would be great together. I've been wondering when you were going to notice how hot he is. The younger man thing is very chic these days. But take it slow this time—enjoy the ride. Flirt with him, keep it light. You've been through a lot, honey. Do you want some coffee? I can make some."

Iris shook her head."No thanks. I'm overcaffeinated already. Luc did seem interested in the catering idea though."

"I thought you already hired *A Dash of Salt* to do the dinner."

"No, they were going to make us pick between two menus, both of which sounded like church suppers. And the other caterer seemed too crunchy granola. Imagine the flack I'll get from our classmates if I choose a lousy caterer. Why did I let Norman talk me into taking on this thankless task? He was acting so helpless."

"Yeah, helpless, except when he's running a multi-billion-dollar corporation."

"Right. I must have sucker written on my forehead."

Ellie peered at her friend's face. "Well, look at that. But it sounds like Luc will save your ass with the catering. The food critics have been raving about his cooking. Stop letting these classmates intimidate you, Iris. They're as insecure as you are."

"Gee, thanks. That makes me feel all bonded with them. At least I'll have an excuse to spend some time with Luc."

"But as his employer—not such a good dynamic. remember my advice—keep it light and slow."

"Keep *what* light and slow? I will bow to your wisdom, O Dating Coach."

CHAPTER 7

Adam Lincoln slid the collapsible stool into his duffel, grabbed his 'old fart' cap off the hall console, and rested his hand on the doorknob. "I'm going out," he shouted into the reverberating void of his New York City condo.

"Wait," Alyssa's mules scuffled on the parquet. "Where are you going?" She trained her sights on the wooden legs sticking out of his bag and exuded disapproval. "Darling, don't you think that's a bit of a time sink?"

"No more so than your book club."

"Fine. But be sure to get back in time to clean up before dinner. We're going out tonight." She flounced back to the living room where she had been deep into the May issue of Vogue.

Adam hurried along the limestone cavern of West 91st Street, headed south for a block down Central Park

West, then cut into the park. He followed a path tracing the northern side of the Reservoir until he came to a slight rise. He slowed down to stretch out the moment before he'd see it through the trees—this perfect piece of poetry. It made his skin prickle. Calvert Vaux's mastery had created a testament to the Gothic Revival movement 150 years ago. Adam had never seen another bridge that could touch it. Well, maybe in Venice. The cinquefoil design on the handrail resembled delicate lace, and the cast iron spandrels somersaulted into an oval vault for the lower level of bridal path to pass through. He wandered around searching for the perfect vantage point, one that put the bending tree that echoed the bridge's arch in the foreground, then planted himself on the stool. It was chilly out here for early May. He zipped up his fleece to his chin.

He retrieved his easel and screwed it into a flat position, hooking on his water cup and paint attachment tray. Next, he unrolled the tissue paper around his brushes, Kolinsky Sable all the way from Siberia, the best. Calvert Vaux had been a watercolorist as well as an architect, like him. But Adam could never hope to lay claim to creations like this bridge. Still, stacked up in boxes in his building's basement storage cage were 214 watercolor paintings of this bridge in different seasons and light conditions. Today the tally would reach 215. He was the J.M.W. Turner of Central Park. That was a laugh. If he could only manage to capture a fraction of the deftness of this bridge he would hang up his brushes.

"Maybe you should just paint and forget trying to be an architect." Those words were lodged in his brain like a tormenting pebble in a shoe.

***

Alyssa Lincoln listened idly to Adam's voice cutting through the background jazz at New York City's fabled Monkey Bar. He was always in such a bad mood after his painting sessions.

"That Norman is such an asshole. He's having this reunion dinner at his fancy new house just to rub our noses in the fact that he's loaded and we're not. And that bitch, Iris Reid—how did she get to be his architect? She was never a great designer. Norman didn't even like her in school." Adam glared at one of the life-sized jazz figures on the mural facing him.

"Maybe she slept with him. Ugh. No, I can't imagine her being that desperate for work. Besides, she inherited that fantastic house from her parents, so she probably doesn't even have a mortgage." She shrugged as she rooted around her plate for the last bits of lobster. *New York Magazine* is right. They do have the best seafood salad here. "Some people evidently get things handed to them in life."

"Remind me again why we have to go to this thing."

"What thing?"

"The reunion—we were just talking about it!"

"I told you, Adam—I want G.B. to give me a teaching job at GSD next fall. I'm going to go postal if I have to spec one more fabric wall divider at Fansler Interiors. G.B. always liked me."

"He liked me more."

"Good. *You* get him to give me a job. I want to teach a design studio." She twirled the ice in her drink with a monkey stirrer. "I can fly home on weekends, or when the twins are home from college. Or you could fly up. I'll get a cute apartment near Harvard Square."

"Uh, 'Lyssa, I don't think people start out teaching at Harvard. I think you have to work your way up—unless you're famous."

"Darling, when have I ever followed the conventional route to getting ahead?"

***

"Now, tummies on the mat for swimming, ladies. Oh, and Gill too, sorry," shouted the sadist-in-lycra.

It's Gilles, not Gill, you twit, thought G.B. He could not believe that this was his life, here, in a gym—or spa, or whatever they called them now. His T.A., Steve, had insisted that Pilates would tighten G.B.'s abs and solve his throbbing back issues. God knew Steve's abs looked solid enough.

"Okay—shoulders and legs off the mat as we begin our flutter kick!"

G.B. had picked this class in the Back Bay, a short walk from his Beacon Hill townhouse, so as not to run into anyone he knew. He shot a quick sideways glance at the pony-tailed forty-something next to him energetically waving her feet up and down, toned arms suspended six inches above the mat. Trophy wife, natch. God, his stomach was burning already. He peeked at his watch. *Merde*—another forty minutes.

"Gimme twenty more kicks. Lookin' good!"

The added advantage of going to this class, beyond admiring the tulips carpeting the Boston Garden on his walk over, or cruising the sales at Bilzerian's on Newbury Street afterward, was that it delayed his checking Steve's blog every morning. He would take this damn class all week and wean himself off its gravitational pull. Who had invented this blogging business anyway? Why would anyone want to expose himself—chatter away about what he had done the night before, what movies he was watching, who he was doing things with? It was bizarrely fascinating. But he had already deleted it from his bookmarks bar. And he'd be buff for the reunion next month. Let's not forget that goal, Gilles Reynard Guillaume Broussard. He might seem like a fossil to his present students, and to Steve, but to his coterie from the class of 1988, he was still their charismatic, brilliant leader. And they were all coming—all ten from his third-year design studio. He took it as a personal victory. Of course he'd had to do a bit of nudging.

"Gill, if you're tired, just go into child pose and wait for us. Only do what your body allows. Reflect on your life's journey. Five more!"

He'd kill for a cigarette. He'd call Jerry after he got out of here and get him to stay at the townhouse during the reunion. He missed having company.

"Okay, on your backs now for knee-to-alternate-elbows!"

G.B. groaned and rolled over. As he lifted his shoulders slightly, elbow extended tentatively, the pilates Nazi strolled over and slipped her cold hand under his lower back.

"Lift from the waist, Gill. Isn't that better?"

No, it hurts a lot more, actually. He bared his teeth at her. Why hadn't they come back to earlier reunions—his chickadees, his favorite class? He sighed. It was that party—the tragedy at that party. And the poor, sweet boy. The brilliant, attractive boy. Why did he have to die?

***

The stylish, late-century Modern offices of Jensen/Dewitt/Twitty were located on the twentieth floor of a Wacker Drive skyscraper, affording Jerry Jensen a premium view of the Chicago River. He watched a team of rowers. Or were they called scullers? The one facing forward had on a sleeveless shirt.

He jumped as his intercom made its irritating mosquito-buzzing sound, then barked into the box, "Who is it, Meg?"

As usual, this latest assistant side-stepped the relevant information. "There's a call on one for you, Mr. Jensen." Where did his office manager find these ninnies? He slipped into his Aeron chair and punched a button.

A voice purred, "I have been hearing some colorful rumors about you. Tell me that the one in the Apollo Theater was not true."

Recognizing the voice, Jerry braced himself for a skirmish. "Things getting boring in Beantown, G.B.? You need a vicarious thrill by reviewing my antics?"

"I miss our fervent chats. Come visit me."

Jerry aligned the files on his glass desk. "My, aren't we waxing nostalgic. I seem to recall a rather unpleasant visit last time."

"Oh that. You are not going to hold that against me forever, are you? Let me atone."

Jerry was relishing the present power reversal. He knew how to work a silence.

"I see that you are coming for the reunion in June. You should stay with me."

Jerry loved forcing G.B.'s cards onto the table so soon. "I'll be returning to the fold to rebond with my fellow narcissistic phonies. I don't think that I should sequester myself with you. Been there, done that. "

There was a pause. "Did you notice that I convinced Will to come?"

Jerry hesitated. Damn G.B. for remembering his Achilles heel. The memory of staring fixedly at the back of Will's glorious wavy hair during structures class popped into his head unbidden. Will had always been catnip for him. "Who else is coming?" He asked trying to muddy the waters.

"Well, Alyssa and Adam, your class's Heloise and Abelard will be there, of course. And Norman Meeker is acting as pukka-sahib, having the Friday dinner at his new house designed by Iris Reid."

"Ugh, Will's girl-toy. So, we'll have lust, pride, sloth, envy, and wrath?"

"Oh, and C.C. promised to come. Maybe you can pedal some project to her—write off the trip."

"Great. There's gluttony! But you know that cuttingedgedecor doesn't publish commercial architecture."

"Well, your reimbursibles department will not know that."

"Hmm. That's true. Good idea. It's been awhile since I've seen the old gang. I'll have to think about your offer of hospitality. Au revoir."

He hung up, then flipped open his laptop. After pressing some keys, an image appeared of a glass-walled Modernist living room floating high above an expanse of water. He scrolled through the rest of the photos in the listing. The light in the spaces was amazing.

He pressed a speed dial number on his cell-phone.

"Hi, Tony. It's Jerry Jensen. Is that condo you showed me on Lake Shore Drive still available?"

"Oh, hi Jerry. Yeah, it's still there. The seller doesn't want to come down at all from the asking, so in this economy it should be there awhile. But... you never know."

"Good. I'm still interested, but can't make an offer for another month. Keep me informed if anyone makes a move on it, all right?"

"Sure. I want you to get it. Call me once you know that your financing is ready to go. Then we can move fast."

Jerry tapped his pen on the desk and thought to himself. Time for Norman Meeker Enterprises to commission a new headquarters.

***

In Berkeley, California, Will Reynolds bobbled his head as he tapped out the drum solo to "In a gadda-da-vida" with two felt-tipped pens on the edge of his side table. He finished with a flourish, then spun his chair around toward the computer to reassure himself that the numbers hadn't changed during his recital. Renno baby, your ship has come in! He stood up to peer over the workstation walls of the factory loft that he and his partner had converted into an architecture office. Everyone had gone to lunch, except one overly conscientious assistant, Traci, who was hunched over her computer.

Will lounged against her partition wall. "Hey, Trace, aren't you gonna break for lunch?" He flashed her a boyish grin. "You work too hard."

She gazed up at him over her black nerd glasses. "Vanessa needs these specs redone for her 3:00 meeting. I brought in a salad for lunch. I'm on a diet."

He leaned in close to let her get a whiff of his aftershave. "I was hoping to buy you a large iced mochaccino in exchange for you bringing me one. How about it?"

Traci snapped her gum and weighed her options. "Okay."

After making sure that she was out of earshot, Will raced back to his desk, snapped on his blue tooth headset, and punched in a phone number. "Hey C.C., it's me, Will. What are you doing? Can you talk?"

"Go away—you're interfering with my on-line shopping time. There's a shoe sale on the Bergdorf's website and I see some Jimmy Choo boots with my name on them."

He heard the sound of tapping.

"Okay, I ordered them. Now you have my attention."

"I'm calling about the reunion. G.B. Rasputin called and put the screws on me to come. I can't believe he hasn't found new victims by now to manipulate."

"I'm sure he has. We were just his 'first.' You never forget your 'first.' He got to me too and I wasn't even one of his boys. I agreed to go to the Friday dinner. But it's okay. I want to see your old girlfriend's house for Norman. I may publish it. So what did you want to ask me about?"

"Oh, shit, Iris. I'll have to see her again and she hates me."

"I can't imagine why. Besides, it's been twenty years. I think you're flattering yourself."

"Never mind. That's not why I called. Have you kept up with Norman at all? I mean personally? We've all read the articles."

"No, can't say that I've clamped eyes on Mr. Insufferable since we graduated. Why?"

"An old school in the Mission section of San Francisco's going up for auction. I've got to get my hands on it. It's perfect for condos. I've already figured out the design work and put together the numbers. There's tons of asbestos. That'll scare away the other developers, but we can get the guys in the space suits to dispose of that. I just need an investor. The Bank turned me down, ass-holes. Hey, you and Sarah don't have a few mil to invest in a good deal, do you?"

"Ri-i-i-ight, dream on, bud."

"Just giving you first crack. According to Fortune Magazine, Norman has more money than he can use in this lifetime, so do you think he'd back me on this condo deal? Should I ask him during the reunion when he's feeling nostalgic for his old classmates?"

"You mean because we were so nice to him?"

"We were nice enough. He was a pompous ass back then. So, do you think I should hit him up? I think I've got some leverage to make him take me seriously."

"Is this project going to be 'green'? Never mind, it won't be ready in time."

"So should I talk to Norman about it?"

"I guess it can't hurt to ask."

***

"Now this is what I call a marketable talent," C.C. squeezed her eyes shut.

"Yeah. My Craig's List ad could read—Missy Shiatsu—your feet in my lap," Sarah smirked. In fact, C.C.'s feet were resting in her lap at that moment as they shared the L-shaped leather sectional. The shiatsu course Sarah had taken the previous winter at the New School had turned out to be a good investment.

"God, are you tense!" Sarah's brow puckered as she kneaded the areas below C.C.'s baby toes. "Is it the news about Met Home?"

"I swear I'm getting an ulcer. I keep waiting for Paul to haul me in to his office. All the other 'shelter porn' magazines seem to be going down like dominos." She gazed out the huge windows as the violet dusk deepened into the black of the Hudson River. She loved this loft. She had found it before the Meatpacking District had taken off, and had bought it for a song. Then, during the renovation, she had met Sarah who was working as a finish carpenter on her contractor's crew. That was when her life had made a U-turn toward a contentment she had never expected. Now, if she lost her job, would Sarah stay with her without the prestige of her work, or the perks that came with it? How would she be able to afford her Manhattan lifestyle?

"That's not going to happen to cuttingedgedecor, baby. Your publishers have deeper pockets. They'll probably scoop up some of those orphan Met Home advertisers. It'll be okay."

"Well, I'm trying to pull together that September issue on green architecture. It's Paul's pet project. Which reminds me—I've got to go to that damned reunion so I can see this wonder house that Iris designed for Norman. I hear from G.B. that it's got all the latest eco-bells and whistles. Are you sure you don't want to come with me? Will's going to be there. He called me today at the office."

"Why is he going to a reunion after all these years? No, I'd better not go. After what you've told me about how nasty some of these people were to you back then, I'm afraid I might punch out somebody's lights."

"I may need you to help *me* behave. I forget why Will said he was going. I'll ask him next month. What is that area you're massaging now?"

"Here? Right by the ball of the foot?"

"Yeah, it kind of hurts."

"That's because it corresponds to your liver, where all those martinis are wreaking havoc."

With that reminder, C.C. downed the rest of her drink.

CHAPTER 8

Five weeks later Norman sat in his office on the top floor of Norman Meeker Enterprises, behind his Danish, blond-wood desk, clumsy fingers setting his 'executive toy' stainless steel balls in motion, back and forth, back and forth.

"Claire! Has she called?"

His assistant stuck her head in the door. "She's only 15 minutes late, Norman. It's a monsoon out there. She'll need an ark to get here."

At that moment the outer door clicked open, and Iris Reid greeted Claire as she edged in past her. Realizing that her umbrella was dripping on the Berber carpet, Iris retreated to park it in the umbrella stand and returned.

"Sorry I'm late. Storrow Drive is closed near the B-School." She dropped down into the guest chair, pulled a clipboard out of her over-sized tote, and passed him a revised chart of the schedule.

"Assuming that this rain lets up—which it's supposed to do tomorrow—we should be in pretty good shape, Norman. The painters are scheduled to start on Monday. The floor finishers will come afterward. We should be able to complete everything in three more weeks. There might be some punch list items to deal with after the party, but nothing noticeable will be missing."

"I hope not, Iris. Remember, I want to knock C.C.'s socks off at this dinner." For what it cost to build I deserve to get some premium PR out of this house. He had chosen Iris as his architect despite suspecting she didn't like him. He never would have considered using a stranger. And the others from the class were designing skyscrapers or museums, while she had lasered in on residential design—the latest materials, eco-conscious approaches, practical nitty-gritty, and most important to him now, how to design a magazine-cover-worthy house.

"Here are the latest requisitions from Farraday. I've checked them all and they're ready to be paid. I've included my latest invoice in there too."

Norman put on his wire-rimmed glasses and pretended to study the top page. This was phase two of his plan. His ex-wife, Barb, had been part of phase one. He had picked her out of that snooty class to stand by him while he built up an empire. She had shared those years of slogging through business school while trying to develop environmental products on the side. But Barb couldn't see the big picture. Not to mention that she'd turned into a bitch. It wasn't only about money or security. Most of the jerks in his GSD class had acquired a kind of polish merely by coming through the friggin' birth canal. Take Iris Reid—typical WASP from some academic family. Sure, she tried to dress edgy with her black leather jacket and boots. But anyone could see, from her porcelain skin and boarding-school accent that she was a good girl from the right side of the tracks. Shit—architecture was 'a gentleman's profession.' You were supposed to go into it for the love of it, not the money. What a bunch of chumps. What had he been thinking spending three years there? Business school had made a lot more sense.

"Do you see a problem, Norman? You're frowning."

"No, no." Norman leaned back in his ergonomic chair. "I'll have Claire cut the checks."

***

The meeting finally over, Iris battled her way through the slashing rain to her Jeep. As soon as she'd buckled her seat belt, her cell phone rang. "Undisclosed caller" appeared on the screen.

"Hi, Iris, it's Will. How are you?" She froze at the sound of his voice and, covering the mouthpiece, forced herself to take several deep breaths.

"I'm fine. I noticed on the GSD website that you're coming to the reunion." God, now she sounded perky.

"Yeah. I have to be in New York on business the week after, so I figured I'd stop off in Cambridge for the weekend. Maybe we could get together for coffee before this thing starts? It's been a long time since we've talked and things kind of blew up at the end of school. I've always felt bad about that."

She tried to figure out what she wanted to happen. "I'm going to be pretty busy on Friday afternoon. Norman's got me running around organizing everything for the dinner. I'll probably be out in Lincoln at the house." She wouldn't make it too easy for him.

"I heard that you designed a house for Norman. I can't wait to see it."

"Well, I guess if you can get yourself out there in the afternoon, we could meet then. I'll be there until five or so. Then I'll need to go home to change."

"Okay. I'll take an early flight and find you in Lincoln. Norman sent directions in the reunion package. Maybe you can give me a tour."

"Sure. See you." Damn. So much for playing hard to get...

CHAPTER 9

It was D-Day and counting. The floor finishers and touch-up painters performed a careful ballet during the week leading up to the party. The day before, gardeners had planted vegetation on the roof and Iris' crew had set the furniture in place following her floor plans. Several full-grown maples had been planted to frame the view of the open field from the living room windows.

Now, as the cleaning crew packed up their equipment, Iris lugged in a large bucket of white peonies and chartreuse lady's mantle chosen that morning from a Harvard Square florist. She set to work arranging them in two Aalto vases on the dining table, making sure that they were low enough not to block the guests' views of each other.

She had written out ten place-cards and was slotting each one down into silver Elsa Peretti holders when she heard a car drive up. Shoving back her sweater sleeve, she consulted her watch—4:15. Will?

But, a few moments later, it was Luc's shaggy head that popped inside the door.

"Hi, you," he said, his arms loaded with bags.

"Can I help? The kitchen's that-a-way," she pointed with her head.

"Thanks. There are two more bags in the car."

She brought in the remaining supplies and joined him at the kitchen island where he was unpacking containers of different shapes and sizes. He moved around the kitchen like a dancer, clad in black jeans and a navy T-shirt, looking relaxed and in control. She settled onto a stool to watch.

"Are you here to be my sous-chef?" he asked, wrapping the strings of a white apron around his narrow hips.

"I'm just getting the table ready. I'll need to head home soon to change. The red wine's on that counter and the white and champagne are in the fridge. Where are your helpers?"

"I don't need helpers to cook for a ten-person party, but Louise is coming to help serve and clean up. Why don't you open some wine for us and keep me company while I prep?" He started slicing lemons.

"I can stay awhile. I chose an Albino Armani pinot grigio to go with the bronzino. Should I open that?"

"Sounds like you run a soup-to-nuts operation if you even choose the wine for your clients. By the way, I love this house. I walked around outside before I came in. It's sort of a Fallingwater meets Neutra."

"Well, aren't you the Renaissance guy? Where did you learn about architecture?"

"Oh, we chef/restauranteurs try to keep up." There went his left dimple.

Iris swirled the wine in her glass and inhaled. "A pretty nose…"

He looked up at her and cocked his head.

She took a sip. "Mmmm. Subtle and fruity, but what's that teaser? A bit of pear on the mid-palate? Sorry. I love good wine."

"Impressive! If you cook too I'm going to be totally intimidated."

Butter started crackling in a big stainless steel pan on the professional range. Luc began shaking Arborio rice into it. As he trickled in some broth from one of his containers, Iris watched him from behind, sipping her wine. Such strong arms. Did hefting crates of produce do that?

"I'm more of a baker," she told him. "Ellie's daughter, Raven, is my best fan. She'll be home from college soon so I'll need to whip up her favorite cake— a Lady Baltimore."

"An architect, a wine aficionada, and a baker. Now I am impressed."

Over the last month Iris found that they had developed an easy rapport even if it had stopped short of romance.

"Should I fill you in on the cast tonight? You're doubling as my bodyguard, remember?"

"Of course. Now, this guy Norman. He's going to live in this house by himself?"

"Yup. He's newly divorced, so this will be his swinging bachelor pad. He's in a furnished apartment at the Devonshire now and plans to move here next week now that construction is done."

"Oh, and Ellie mentioned that your old boyfriend is coming." There was a loud sizzling as he poured in more broth, continuing to stir with a wooden spoon.

"Yeah—Will. He'd said he was going to stop by here this afternoon, but hasn't shown up. That's typical of him, actually. If he comes by in the next hour, you should feel free, as my bodyguard, to rip out his still-beating heart."

"Ended badly, did it?"

"You could say that." Iris frowned, then hurried on. "Continuing on with the cast of characters, Ellie's bringing her husband, Mack—a great guy. I don't think you've met him, have you? He's a doctor, very laid back."

"I don't usually think of doctors as laid back. Could you hand me that mitt, please?"

"He's a pediatrician. You'll like him. However, on the unlikable side, we have Alyssa and Adam, the class couple. She's a prima donna. She and Adam married after graduation. But the *male* Alpha role goes to our professor, Gilles Broussard, known as G.B. He's kind of a self-appointed guru."

"That's a little weird—only one professor coming?"

"He was the professor for this group's third-year studio and the Friday night dinners are divided up by studios. He's also been helping Norman organize the reunion."

"So," Luc raised his hands. He lowered fingers one by one as he counted "that's you, Ellie, her husband, Norman, the old boyfriend, the prom king and queen, and the Professor. Who are the last two?"

"I've saved the scariest two for last. You can't miss C.C. Okuyama. She's built like a Sherman tank with the face and voice of Babe Ruth. She's an editor from cuttingedgedecor who's interested in publishing a piece on this house. Norman will be pestering her all weekend to do just that, but C.C. asked me not to tell him that she's already interested. I think she likes torturing him."

"How charming. But the publishing part—that would be great for you, wouldn't it?" Luc looked up from the simmering broth.

"Sure. My career could always use the boost. I'm terrible at marketing. But Norman wouldn't be doing this for me. He's trying to repackage himself as a cool dude, living in a hip house from a magazine. It's part of a whole fantasy he's trying to create."

"I can't wait to finally meet this guy, Norman. He sounds like a trip. But hang on—who's the tenth person?"

"I almost forgot our phantom—Jerry Jensen. Everything about him is beige—hair, skin, even his eyes—well, they're light brown. He even wore a lot of khaki at school. Only his sarcastic smirk stands out. He reminds me of the Cheshire Cat in 'Alice in Wonderland', all grin and nothing to get a handle on."

"He sounds almost innocent compared to the rest."

"Oh no, no one would ever accuse Jerry of innocence." Iris stared into her glass and swirled the golden liquid gently. "There was someone else in our class who was unusual." She told Luc about Carey and about her vow with Ellie to try to figure out who had killed him.

At the start of the story, Luc turned the burner to its lowest setting and sat down on a stool to listen. After she finished he stood up and came closer. She stood up and he wrapped her in his arms.

After a minute he looked down at her and said "God, with classmates like these, one even capable of murder, how did you survive?"

"Not all of us did."

CHAPTER 10

Someone—Alyssa no doubt—had decided that black tie would be "fun." Instead of following directions, Iris squirmed into a slinky, bronze, above-the-knee dress. She sucked on a Tic-Tac as she wound her hair up and plunged a dragonfly comb through it like a saber. After smudging her eyeliner and retouching her lipstick, she slid on leopard-patterned heels. You babe, she thought as she inspected herself in the full-length mirror. Twenty years ago she had fit the term 'coltish.' Now what was she—'mare-ish'? A little rounder, more filled out—but still capable of a full gallop.

Driving back out to Lincoln, she fretted about the prospect of making small talk that night. She hated social occasions—and this one was going to be a minefield. This was no soft, fuzzy crowd. They would be scrutinizing her and analyzing Norman's house for perceived "mistakes." She marveled at Ellie's ability to ride the top of a conversational wave—to view tonight's party as dinner theater. Why couldn't Iris care less? These were people she couldn't stand—and one of them was almost certainly her friend's killer. Last night, she had made Ellie promise not to be late for the cocktail hour so she wouldn't be stranded with them for long.

She backed her car into a spot that would allow for a quick exit. The evening felt chilly for early June. While hobbling up the pea gravel driveway, she regretted choosing three-inch heels.

Through the door's sidelights she could see Norman's silhouette hurrying toward her. The expression on his face as he approached displayed obvious relief. He jerked forward to deliver an awkward peck nearly on her cheek. "Where have you been? They'll be arriving any minute!"

"Don't you look nice, Norman." A well-cut tux could hide a multitude of sins.

She moved around the hall and living room, adjusting the lighting to produce a soft glow, then stacked eight Brazilian jazz CDs, brought from her collection, into the embarrassingly expensive sound system. Satisfied, she scanned the room. The stage was set.

"Did Will turn up?" she asked Norman who was looking in the front hall mirror, fiddling with his bow tie.

"No, I haven't seen him. Isn't he coming with the others?"

"We'd made a plan to meet here before five while I was getting the house ready. Maybe his plane got delayed."

"I've been here since 5:30 and didn't get a call from him here or on my cell. I'm sure he'll show up."

"He probably just blew off the meeting with me and will show up for the dinner," she said lightly, inwardly fuming.

The doorbell startled them.

G.B. and Jerry arrived together. Norman morphed into host mode, pumping their hands and making welcoming noises. Jerry gave Iris a wave and smirk. G. B., more gallant, air-kissed her on either check. Iris was not a kisser, air or otherwise. She flashed her teeth instead and tried to look sincere.

"Oh, my dears. Look at this house. It is magnificent! Iris, I always said you had a gift." He had never said anything of the sort, Iris reflected, watching him glide over to the windows to admire the view. He slid out his cigarette case and tap, tap, tapped on it.

Who still smoked? Iris couldn't think of anyone but him.

Over the preceding years, Jerry had progressed from boyish to middle-aged, with little change in affect. His pale, lashless eyes watched her impassively, while his lips remained in a tight sneer.

"When did you get in from Chicago, Jerry?" Norman asked.

"I flew in this morning and had lunch with G.B. He seems to have kept tabs on all of us."

Luc, wearing a chambray chef's jacket, entered with a tray of brimming champagne flutes and was met with appreciative stares from G.B. and Jerry. Behind him, Louise carried a tray of potato galettes with Iranian caviar which she offered around. She wore a long, vintage dress of dusty-rose lace and had removed her nose ring for the occasion.

G.B. leaned in toward Luc, "I prefer Grey Goose—rocks and lemon."

A sharp knock drew everyone's attention to the half-open door, and Ellie appeared.

As if following stage instructions, she introduced Mack to the four men, being careful to include Luc.

"G.B. tells me you're a doctor." Jerry had done his homework. It was amazing how much G.B. seemed to know, considering how little overt communication the group had had in 20 years.

Ellie sidled over to Iris and whispered "So, all ready for the Donner expedition?"

The introductory chit-chat went on for another ten minutes, punctuated by rounds of food and drink, until the grand entrance of Alyssa and Adam. Alyssa's little-girl voice preceded them. "I can't believe it! We're all together again. This is so exciting!" Her doll-like features were aglow with pleasure. She still wore her hair shoulder-length in blond curls straight from hot rollers.

Adam was right behind her, carrying two bottles of wine."It's so nice of you to do this, Norman. This house is really something! Oh hi, Iris. Where's Will?"

"Not here yet." Iris' reply was drowned out in the babble of greetings. G.B. hurried up to double-kiss Alyssa, using actual touch this time. He and Adam exchanged awkward embraces.

Next to arrive was C.C., even more tank-like than before, sheathed in a long, gray muu-muu. Her hooded eyes swept the room. She immediately zeroed in on Iris and wagged her finger.

"Uh, oh. Someone didn't get the dress memo. Or is this what passes for black-tie in Cambridge?" she said, surprising Iris with a hug.

"Getting out of our Birkenstocks is black-tie in Cambridge, C.C."

"And where did you find this darling dress? It's so... you."

"It's from Barney's." By way of Filene's Basement. "And yours?"

"Oh, I designed this and had it sewn up the last time I was in Hoi An for the magazine. I swear I spend half my life on Sing Air."

"And they are lucky to have you, C.C. Most of us couldn't fit in all that travel with our busy personal lives," trilled Alyssa, moving in to join them.

Iris stole a look at Alyssa. Her cheekbones looked lifted, as if by a push-up bra.

"And how are those adorable rug-rats of yours, Alyssa? Who says that the Mommy-track precludes all the interesting jobs?" C.C. shot back.

Luc had overheard this last bit of sniping and pivoted around to offer them some miniature crab cakes. He shot Iris a quick wink.

"Adam. You have to try these!" Alyssa called out across the room.

As Luc moved away, C.C. said with a malicious smile, "Looks like our Iris may be having the waiter for dessert."

"Luc's not a waiter. He owns a restaurant and is catering this dinner as a favor to Ellie and me."

"Well, good for you, Iris," Alyssa said ambiguously as she stuffed a galette delicately into her fuschia mouth.

"I'm loving what I'm seeing so far of this house," C.C. said sotto-voce into Iris' ear. "Let's talk after dinner about logistics for a photo-shoot, okay?"

It was going to be a long evening. As Norman led a tour through the house, the group scrutinized the design details and made comments like sharks at a carcass. It took less than ten minutes for someone to insinuate that Iris had stolen the house's design concept from one of their school projects.

"This reminds me of my design for the Ungers studio. Remember that one, Adam?" Alyssa always played the heroine in her own movie, but Adam was too busy mentally tallying up the house's probable construction costs to respond. At that moment, he was filling his phone's camera memory—furtively Iris noted—with photos of Norman's furniture.

"Alyssa, didn't you design a curtain-wall office tower for Ungers' studio?" Jerry dead-panned.

"Well, it had the same parti of stacked elements— sort of cubist, with a lot of transparency." She was clearly oblivious to his frontal assault.

Iris noticed Jerry whisper something into G.B.'s ear, turning away first in case there were lip readers watching him.

"Mack," Ellie called over. "You have to see the master bath. I want Iris to use these tiles in our bathroom."

"Uh oh, are we doing another renovation?" Mack protested as Ellie dragged him away.

Norman sidled over to C.C. and made his annoying little cough to get her attention.

"You know, I let Iris put her name on the design of this house, but I gave her some pretty extensive ideas. I'd love to give you a tour. Remind me, what magazine are you working for these days?"

C.C. graced Norman with a glacial smile and flipped down her cherry-red glasses from their nest atop her helmet of hair. "Oh, Norman, you've left our provincial field of architecture so-o-o far behind. I'm sure that you don't have time to read shelter magazines."

"Well, C.C., someone has to be the patron and keep these innovative architects in business, don't you think?" he intoned, a smile plastered to his face.

G.B. tapped his cheek with a finger as he stared at the windows. Turning around, he spurted out "I'm fascinated with the semiotics of this house, Iris. I will bet that not many people will notice that the pattern of the fenestration follows the proportions of the Fibonacci series. Please explain to me what you are saying with that gesture?"

The corners of her mouth flickered up in a suppressed smile. Norman hadn't noticed that reference. "Let's discuss my concepts over dinner, G.B. I'm seeing Norman signal for us to sit down now."

Iris and Ellie had carefully worked out a seating plan and rehearsed what questions to try to work into the conversations. Ellie was positioned down at Norman's end of the table with Alyssa, G.B. and Adam. Iris was at the other end flanked by C.C. and Jerry with Mack and Will's empty seat beyond.

Before they could begin the meal, Norman stood up to give a toast. He started off with "this was always a very special class," and went on to enumerate every funny or embarrassing memory he could dredge up. People resignedly put their glasses back down on the table. Iris' mind wandered off as he segued into a narrative of the classmates' various accomplishments, oh-so-modestly leaving out his own.

Iris studied Adam's face in profile. Unlike his wife, he hadn't aged well. There was something slack about his features. It looked as if Alyssa had sucked out all of his life-force.

Louise peeked in twice from the kitchen to see if she could serve the salad. Norman, however, was jammed on transmit.

Finally, in a rare display of practicality, G.B. rose, glass in hand, and cut off Norman in mid-gauzy-sentiment. "Here's to Norman who has generously opened up his lovely new home to us all. Bravo!"

Everyone rose immediately, raising their glasses and crying out "Bravo!" to keep Norman from starting up again in response. They all sat down and Louise swept in with the salads before anything could stop her.

Iris overheard fragments of conversations throughout the many courses. C.C. was energetically telling Jerry about a photo shoot in Chicago gone horribly awry, her uni-bosom shelved on the table. His glazed smile said *you really are repulsive,* while his lips said "how amusing for you."

G.B. held court with Norman and Adam, trying to convince them to get more involved with their alma mater, perhaps by participating on design juries now that they were 'respected professionals.' Norman and Adam sported the folded-armed, steely expression of men-who-will-not-be-corralled.

Alyssa had commandeered the patient Ellie, who was, in turn, trying to steer the talk back to her own agenda. At one point, Alyssa's high-pitched voice broke through a momentary lull in the conversation, "and we had to wait around for two days after the graduation party for that investigation to end. We almost missed our plane to Florence." In the candlelight, even her eyes seemed to pout.

Ellie caught Iris' eyes and slugged back the remaining wine in her glass. Immediately animated conversations broke out on any subject but the long-ago graduation party or Carey's death.

Iris sighed. She hadn't been able to get C.C. or Jerry to go near those topics. She figured she might as well chat with Mack about how to keep deadly nightshade from taking over her garden. That at least was useful information. She and Ellie could regroup after dinner and decide if they would go to any more of the scheduled events.

But just as Louise brought in the apricot tart with lavender ice cream, the harsh sound of the front bell froze a half-dozen witty exchanges mid-repartee.

Adam broke the silence. "It must be Will! He loves to make a dramatic entrance."

Eight sets of eyes followed Norman as he scurried to the adjacent entry hall. Alyssa jumped up and followed him as far as the framed opening, with Adam tagging behind. Everyone else craned their necks to get a better view. Norman opened the door to two men in dark clothes. Eight sets of ears tuned in.

"Hello. I'm Detective Paul Malone of the Cambridge Major Crimes Division and this is Detective Connors." A tall, scarecrow of a man in an ill-fitting sports jacket tipped his head at a shorter man and they both indicated the gold badges on their belts. "Sorry to interrupt your party. Are you Norman Meeker, the owner of this residence?"

The color in Norman's face leached away and he looked unsure whether he should admit to his name.

"Is Iris Reid one of your guests, Mr. Meeker?"

Norman found his voice. "Uh…" Iris approached the door.

"I'm Iris Reid. What's this about, Detective?"

"Do you know a William Reynolds, Ms. Reid?"

"What's wrong? Did something happen to him? He called me from California last week and wanted to meet today. But he never showed up."

At this point, Alyssa appeared at the door. "What's happened to Will? We're having a reunion and he's supposed to be here."

"Yeah, where's Will? Has there been an accident?" Adam spoke from above his wife's head.

Next came G.B. "I'm Professor Broussard, Officers. Perhaps you could fill us all in on what has happened."

Malone looked like a no-bullshit type of guy. He'd probably been called out from Cambridge after his shift had ended to try to get information from some people at a fancy dinner party in Lincoln. He did not look happy.

He ran his hand though his thinning hair and said "All of you, please go back to the dining room. We intend to speak with everyone. Not you, Ms. Reid. You stay with me. Connors, get statements from everyone. Find out if anyone saw Mr. Reynolds after he landed at Logan."

As Connors herded his charges back to the dining table, Malone steered Iris into the living room area, trying to find some privacy—not an easy task in an open plan house.

"I'm sorry to have to tell you this, Ms. Reid, but we discovered Mr. Reynold's body an hour ago. We called his wife in California, and she said that he took the red-eye last night, had plans to meet with you, and then come out here for this dinner."

Alyssa's wail rang through the space, "Oh, no—Will is DEAD! How could he be DEAD? Why would anyone want to kill him?"

Iris and the detective looked over at the faces, white in the glow of the candles. They could hear Connors trying to establish control as Adam moved in to contend with his force field of a wife.

"Wait—you said you found his body?" Iris asked. "Was he mugged?"

Without answering her question, Malone said, "We would appreciate you coming down with us to the station to help us with our investigation." He enunciated each word as if speaking in code. "I'm sorry to break things up here."

"Am I under arrest?" Iris felt the need for a de-coder ring.

"No, no, nothing like that. We'd like for you to identify the body. His wife won't be here until tomorrow. I hope it's not too much of an inconvenience," he added as if this was the last thing he cared about.

Iris looked over to see Luc standing at the door to the kitchen. He was asking her a question with his eyes.

She looked back at him bleakly. Identify the body? Why her? But all she wanted, at that point, was to get out of there. If that meant going with this detective, she'd go.

Malone muttered under his breath "of course, a chef." Louder he said "Anyone else in there? Maybe a butler or a chauffeur?"

Louise peeked from behind Luc. "Just me."

"Go sit in there with the others. Connors, two more," he yelled over.

As Iris was collecting her purse from the entry closet, Ellie and Mack came up behind her. "We're coming with you, Iris. Detective Malone, you can take our statements down at the station."

CHAPTER 11

Iris braced herself and dialed the number for her brother, Stirling. Her sister-in-law, Leesa, answered with, "He's in the middle of *'Law and Order,'* Iris. Is this important?"

"Please tell him that I need him for a real-life episode. I'm down here at the Cambridge Police Station being asked questions about a dead friend."

Stirling's voice came on, "Good God, Iris. What have you gotten yourself into now?" She could visualize the constipated look on his face.

"I've done nothing wrong, Stirling. The police showed up at my Harvard Reunion and said they'd found Will Reynolds' body this afternoon. Will had called me last week and wanted to meet today, so the police seem to think that I know something about his death. But I haven't seen him in 20 years."

"These things never happen at my Yale reunions. Okay, okay, have you said anything to the police?"

" Just that Will never showed up."

"Don't say anything else. Is it the new station in Kendall Square? I'll drive in now."

Iris felt relief at having her brother come to her aid. No one messed with Stirling Reid. He was her only immediate family, so she put up with his pomposity. For once, it might work in her favor.

After Stirling agreed to drive in from Concord, Ellie and Mack, statements signed, went home.

She sat in the tiny interview room with Detective Connors, the second-in-command. It must feel pretty crowded in here when two detectives, a sweating perp and a lawyer were all jammed in together.

Her eyes kept going to the one-way glass. Were there people on the other side watching her every twitch?

"Nice building," she said to Detective Connors to break the silence.

"We just moved over here from Central Square last month. We're still getting used to it." He was consulting his laptop, probably checking her criminal history. He scowled. Had he discovered that "failure to stop" citation from last year? With his bald head and thick neck he resembled a sleek seal, she thought.

Ten minutes later, her big brother and Detective Malone bustled in and placed themselves on opposite sides of the table. Stirling was wearing a suit and wingtips, as if this were how he always dressed for a Friday evening at home. Maybe it was. Stirling nodded loftily to Detective Malone to begin, and Detective

Connors flipped on a wall switch to start the recorder, noting all present.

"Ms. Reid, did you ever call Mr. Reynolds on his cell phone?"

"No, I never called him at all. He called me..."

"Just answer 'yes' or 'no,' Iris," Stirling interrupted.

"Did you know what flight he would be on?"

"No."

"How had you planned to meet up?"

She looked at Stirling, wondering how she was supposed to answer that one with a "yes" or "no." He gave her a nod.

"He said that he'd stop by Mr. Meeker's house in Lincoln in the afternoon because I'd said I would be out there getting things ready for tonight's dinner. Norman had sent out maps showing how to get there. I guess that he was planning to rent a car."

"Don't speculate, Iris," Stirling jumped in.

"What was this meeting supposed to be about?"

Her mind went blank. Why *had* Will wanted to meet with her privately? "I don't know. There wasn't really any agenda. We had dated 20 years ago, then gone our separate ways. I guess Will just wanted to chat before the reunion."

"I understand that it was more serious than just dating. Weren't you two living together during that last year of school? How would you characterize the way things had been left between you and Mr. Reynolds after school ended?"

Iris felt her face flush."We had decided to break up. The relationship wasn't working out."

"Any particular reason?"

"Detective, is this ancient history relevant?" Stirling interjected.

"Yes, Counselor, it is. Ms. Reid?"

"We broke up because Will wasn't faithful. I felt that I couldn't trust him."

Shit. Who had Detective Malone been talking to? Who had made her out to be the vengeful, wronged ex-girlfriend?

"What were you doing from eleven this morning until the dinner tonight?"

She thought for a few minutes then ran through her schedule as Detective Connors took notes. When she got to "then I took my dog for a walk at Fresh Pond," the temperature in the room seemed to chill ten degrees.

"Hold on right there. What time was this?"

"Around 1:30 I guess." Iris chewed on her fingernail as Stirling wrote furiously on his legal pad, then underlined something twice.

"What paths did you take at Fresh Pond?"

"We took the main loop around the reservoir. We walk there every afternoon."

"Iris, just answer the question. Nothing more," Stirling admonished her.

"Did you go off that main path at all?" Malone twirled a pen, trying to sound casual.

"No."

"Okay. Continue with your time-line."

"I got home at around three, read my mail and spoke on the phone with my friend Ellie Mckenzie for about 20 minutes." She proceeded with listing her actions right up to "I drove back to Lincoln at six for the dinner."

Then Stirling asked "Lieutenant, other than a relationship that ended two decades ago and a request for my client to meet him, is there anything else that ties William Reynolds to her?"

"As you know, Counselor, we're not here to answer your questions. But since it will be on the news tonight, I guess that I can tell you that Mr. Reynolds' body was found along a path at Fresh Pond. The time of death has been estimated to be between noon and three, right when Ms. Reid just admitted to being in the area."

Iris made a strangled sound. She could visualize the scene all too well. This was not how she had imagined getting to closure with Will. She might actually have been nearby when Will died. Why had he been there? This didn't make any sense.

"Are you saying that Will was murdered?"

"I can't comment on an active investigation, Ms. Reid."

When Detective Malone next tried to hustle Iris down to the morgue to identify the body, Stirling raised himself to his full height and announced that, as Iris was not a Reynolds family member, she was under no obligation to go through that stress. He was advising her not to do so, reminding the Detective that Iris had come there voluntarily to answer their questions.

Malone knew when he was facing a brick wall and settled for a signature on her sworn statement, finishing up with the cliche not to leave town.

Outside at the curb she turned to her brother and moaned, "Stirling, this can't be happening. Why would anyone want Will dead? The police can't possibly believe that I killed him, can they?"

"Iris, listen carefully. You've admitted that Will screwed around on you when you were together, giving you a possible motive to want him dead. You've admitted that you had a plan to meet him this afternoon. You've admitted to being in the area where his body was found around the time of death. Of course he was murdered. Of course you're a serious suspect. You have motive and opportunity. All they need is means. Still, stewing over an ex-boyfriend's sins for 20 years seems far-fetched, and we don't know what method was actually used. But if one more connection turns up between you and Will, there could be enough circumstantial evidence to get you arrested. You can only hope that a more likely suspect turns up. As a side note, being seen as a murder suspect could be very bad for your business, not to mention your reputation. Or mine, for that matter."

Stirling beeped open his car. "You have your Jeep here, right?"

For some reason she answered, "Uh huh."

CHAPTER 12

Iris hobbled up Upland Road from the T stop, entered the sanctuary of her house, and peeled off her heels to examine her new blisters. Sheba padded over and licked her face sympathetically. After Iris poured herself a glass of sauvignon blanc, she heaved herself onto the sofa, and flicked the TV remote to the 11 o'clock news. Will's death was the lead story. A pedi-cab driver had discovered the body on a path near the Neville Manor Assisted Living Home, located within the boundaries of the Fresh Pond Reservation. A well-groomed reporter, looking solemn and tense with faux concern, stated that the cause of death had yet to be determined. Iris could see shadowy forms moving around inside the police tent in the background. Thank God the reporter didn't speculate about suspects or persons of interest.

***

On Saturday morning Ellie and Mack bustled in through the kitchen door, pausing to pet Sheba who had scrambled up out of her spot inside the kitchen fireplace to greet them. The dog trailed them to the breakfast table in the sunny bay window and laid her silky snout on Iris' knee, rolling her eyes meaningfully—but without real hope—in the direction of Mack's bakery bag.

"Are you okay, Iris?" Mack asked. "I guess you two weren't exaggerating about this crowd being dangerous." Tempting aromas wafted from the bag he set on the table.

"How are you holding up, darlin'?" Ellie hugged her. "Did Stirling get the police to leave you alone?"

Iris leaned her head on her hands. "This is a complete nightmare but at least they haven't Mirandized me yet. I feel like a magnet for dead bodies. My brother-the-lawyer says that if one more thing turns up incriminating me, the police might arrest me for murder."

"*You*? Oh come on! No one could possibly think that *you* had anything to do with Will's death," Ellie said.

Mack cut in. "Does this mean it was definitely murder? Are the police sure that he didn't just stop at Fresh Pond to stretch his legs, then keel over from a heart attack? Maybe he got a blood clot from the long flight." He arranged peach muffins on one of the square plates Iris had set out.

"They wouldn't tell us how he died, but they were grilling me about my movements yesterday afternoon, so I doubt that his death looked like an accident. The awful part is that I was walking Sheba right there at around the time he died."

"You're kidding! He died near where you walk? Did you hear anything?" Ellie asked while bringing over the French press of coffee.

"It said on the news that it happened on a path up by the nursing home. That's too far off for me to have heard anything. But if I *had* made arrangements to meet him there, I suppose I could have slipped away from the dog-walking path to polish him off."

"And Sheba would have been a witness." The dog looked up at Ellie eagerly. "What about it, girl? Did Iris kill the old boyfriend?"

"This sounds like someone's trying to set you up, Iris. How many people know you walk your dog there every afternoon?" Mack asked as he lifted a chunk of muffin to his mouth.

"I've been thinking about that. Anyone who googled me would find *the Cambridge Chronicle* article about my work on the Fresh Pond advisory committee. I said in the interview that I walk my dog there every afternoon."

"So, it could have been anyone," Mack said.

"Well, anyone who knew of the relationship between Iris and Will, anyone who knew that Will was going to be here this weekend, anyone Will trusted enough to agree to meet with," Ellie pointed out.

"In other words, someone at the dinner last night," Iris said.

There was silence as they finished up the last muffin crumbs. Sheba sighed heavily and flopped back down in her fireplace den.

Finally Mack said "I may have collected a clue last night about Carey's death."

"You didn't tell me this!" Ellie said.

"I was waiting for our debriefing session."

"What is that—Hardy Boys etiquette 101?"

"There were only two of them. They didn't need to wait."

"Enough you two—WHAT IS THE CLUE?"

"After the police came, G.B. got up and moved to your seat, Iris, next to Jerry. When Detective Connors announced that Will's dead body had been found, I heard Jerry whisper to G.B. "It's payback from Carey for the brownie." Mack beamed at them expectantly.

"What? Are you sure that you got that right— the brownie?"

Iris' expression took on a vacant look. "Wait—a—minute. Wait—a—minute. I think I may know what he's referring to. At the graduation party, I remember Will offering Carey a brownie from the refreshment table." She squinched her eyes and tried to remember the scene. "Damn, that must've been how the drugs got into Carey's system. But why? Why would Will want to get Carey high?"

They stared at each other as the wheels turned, then all three spoke at once:

"Will must've wanted him to make a fool of himself after showing everyone up for three endless years."

"If Jerry knew about it, I wonder if any more of them were in on the joke."

"Will must have wanted to get Carey disoriented so he could push him over the balcony."

The last comment came from Mack and the women stared at him.

"Isn't that what we're talking about here—who pushed Carey over?"

"Well, yes, but Will as the murderer? I know he was a complete jerk, but a murderer—someone I slept with?"

Ellie put an arm around her. "We always said it had to be one of them. He's one of our suspects."

"Wait a minute," Mack said. "Ellie, you said that if Jerry knew about the drugging plan, then maybe another of them knew as well. What if getting Carey to eat the brownie was the extent of Will's involvement? What if someone else took advantage of Carey's altered state and did the pushing? After all, someone's now murdered Will. Isn't it more likely that Carey's murderer has killed again?"

"Otherwise, if Jerry was on the right track, and this second murder was to avenge Will's drugging and killing Carey, there's only one person we know who would take it on themself to act as Carey's avenger..."

Iris looked pained. "Yeah, me."

CHAPTER 13

Iris convinced a sullen hotel receptionist to phone up to the three rooms. There were many reunioneers milling about in the lobby, but no one seemed to need immediate attention, so Iris couldn't understand why he was acting so beleaguered. The baby-faced youth dressed in a preppy uniform rolled his eyes after each fruitless call. Okay, she wasn't technically a hotel guest, but she was trying to contact his guests. He didn't know that they wouldn't welcome her call. She'd threatened to round the reception desk herself before the clerk agreed to check their status on his computer screen. At least none of them had checked out.

According to the reunion schedule, if they were following it, the group would be attending what was dubbed 'picnic on the lawn' at GSD at noon, followed by a round-table discussion in the auditorium on

"Unmodernism" led by Roger Barton, the class Boy Scout.

She left the hotel and raced to her Jeep just as a meter maid approached brandishing a ticket pad. Iris smiled triumphantly as she started the engine and squealed out into the congested streets of Harvard Square. She crawled along the dozen blocks toward the GSD, her eyes scanning for another parking place. She should have walked the mile from home or even fed the meter and left her car in the square.

The design of Gund Hall, which housed the Graduate School of Design, made no pretense of fitting into its context. Amid the brick Georgian architecture of the nearby quadrangles, Gund Hall rose as a stand-alone testament to 1960's concrete Brutalism. The building resembled a giant football bleacher with each floor as a rising step. Outside, you entered the building by walking under the giant top step, which rested on tall, skinny columns, an entry that was more menacing than welcoming. Iris hurried through lobby and lunchroom to the back lawn.

She saw a long line of people snaking past Roger Barton, who was punching lunch vouchers and handing out book bags stamped with GSD emblems.

"Hey there, Iris! We missed you this morning at the brunch," he called to her gaily, unaware of her new status as a murder suspect.

As she filled out a name tag, she heard another voice behind her.

"Roger, have you seen G.B. anywhere?"

Iris half-turned to eye a well-built young man with a purposefully clenched jaw.

"I think he's in the auditorium setting up for the symposium, Steve," Roger gestured vaguely.

Iris bustled back into the building after Steve, but instead of following him straight ahead to the lobby she turned left toward the open studio levels. She raced up the open stairs two at a time and out the back of the second floor studio into a deserted hallway. After sprinting down its length, she tried to quiet her ragged breathing and cautiously pushed open the door to the auditorium's balcony. Ducking down to crawl as she reached the balcony's edge, she heard Steve's raised voice below.

"Why didn't you give me some notice? Please—you made me look like a moron. I can't prepare to cover one of your semiotics classes with no advanced warning."

She could barely hear G.B.'s placating response.

"... sorry... it was a... yesterday... never... terribly..." he soothed.

Iris eased back onto her haunches. So, G.B. had blown off teaching his semiotics class the day before. The day that Will was murdered.

"I just need you to understand. You put me in an awkward position."

There was some more indecipherable conversation, then one of Piper Auditorium's enormous doors slammed shut.

Iris backtracked to the hall and took the fire stairs up to the fourth floor administration level. The bulletin board she remembered was still hanging outside the Registrar's office. She scanned the schedule for the architecture classes. Professor Broussard's Semiotic class met on Fridays from one until three. O-kaaay. He's definitely on the suspect list.

Pleased by her discovery, Iris descended to the first floor, prepared to unmask the secrets of the other suspects. She spotted her first quarry sitting on a spread of napkins which had been arranged on the patchy ground under a towering elm. Alyssa's blue sweater and white pants stood out from the sea of black and grey architectural mufti around her.

"Hi, Alyssa. Hello Adam. We didn't get much of a chance to talk last night. Did you have to stay long with the detective?"

Alyssa eyed her warily and snapped "Will was our friend." Adam silently glowered.

"And he was my boyfriend, remember?" Iris parried.

"Well, you're the one the cops hauled off." Adam bit off a piece of his roast beef sandwich with a smug look.

"They wanted me to identify the body. Will and I had both moved on with our lives. I didn't even know the adult Will. But you guys must have kept in touch."

Alyssa's eyes gleamed meanly. "We went to his wedding the year after graduation. He married Rachel Allen from the Registrar's office. But then, with kids and work, we all drifted apart. Our lives are so busy, you know. Or maybe you don't know. You're still single, right?"

"I can't imagine who would want to kill Will," *cuckolded husbands, jilted lovers, Rachel,* "but it probably had to do with Will's life in California. Still, it does seem odd that it happened back here in Cambridge," Iris paused for effect, "so near the setting of Carey's death 20 years ago, the last time this group was all together. I wonder if those two deaths could be related? After all, Will was the one who gave Carey that drugged brownie." Iris was warming to her performance, trying to shake loose some reactions.

"What are you playing at, Iris—you think you're the cops?" Adam practically hissed. Then he stuffed his sandwich wrapper in a brown bag, got to his feet and stalked off. Alyssa scurried after him, turning back to glare at her. "This was supposed to be a fun weekend."

"God forbid I should spoil the fun," Iris returned.

She sat thinking for awhile then surveyed the lawn. She couldn't see C.C. or Jerry, but spotted Patty Kim, a sweet woman who had been friendly with Carey, and wandered toward her.

"Hi, Patty. What are you up to these days?"

"Oh, hi Iris. I'm living in Watertown, working for Sasaki. I saw one of your houses in the Sunday *Globe Magazine*. I really liked it."

Iris felt ashamed of herself. Other than Ellie, she hadn't bothered to stay in touch with the few members of her class that she had liked. They chatted about Norman's house and Patty's three kids. Then Patty brought up the subject of Will.

"I saw on the news that Will Reynolds died on his way to the reunion. I'm so sorry, Iris. I know that you guys had been close."

"It's awful. I still can't believe it. And the strange thing is that thinking about this reunion kept reminding me about Carey's death."

"Ohhhh, me too. Poor Carey. Being back here at GSD, I keep expecting to run into him." She leaned in closer. "You know, I never believed that it was an accident. When the autopsy said that he was stoned, I knew that someone else must have been involved."

"That's what I thought too!" Iris said. "Carey told me he never took drugs—even aspirin. His system was too wired. I told that to the detective in charge, but he didn't want to hear it. In their minds, if a student flew off a balcony, the kid was a druggie. End of story. I remember seeing his family at the funeral. His parents and a sister live somewhere around here. They all wore the same bewildered expression as Carey. It broke my heart. Patty, back at the graduation party, did you notice anyone following Carey into that bedroom with the balcony?"

"No, and I've thought about it again and again. I had gone to the bathroom after he and I were talking and he must have wandered in there then. God, I've wished I could redo those few minutes."

"I know what you mean. And now there's been another death. I keep thinking they must be related. But I don't remember any connection between them, beyond Will remarking on how brilliant Carey was. Can you think of any?"

"Well, they were both in G.B.'s design studio that last term. You were in it too, right? I remember watching the last crit. Everyone else in that group, other than you, seemed to be bristling over all the praise he was getting. It was strange because they were all good designers too. If Carey hadn't been in the same class, one of them would've been the class star."

"Yeah, strange and tragic. Listen, if you think of anything else, maybe something that happened during the party, would you please give me a call? I have a card here somewhere..." She fished one out of her purse.

People around them were getting up and moving into the building. Patty stood up and brushed the crumbs off her skirt. "Are you going in to hear the panel?"

"I don't think so. I'll catch you later, Patty. It's been good to see you again."

By now, most people had wandered inside either to snag a good seat in the auditorium or to look at the lobby-mounted exhibits of work by the reunion class. Iris headed for the lobby. Some foresighted administrator must have stored a sampling of presentation boards from back then for precisely this purpose—to flatter alumni into opening up their checkbooks.

The display brought back a flood of memories. The first presentation was of a Michael Graves knock-off of a housing project—a beautifully painted watercolor of a building that looked like a cartoon. While the structure itself was a half-baked pastiche of post-Modernist clichés, every tree and window mullion had been lovingly rendered. It was Adam's. Iris remembered how excruciating his final review had been, with one critic suggesting he stick to painting watercolors and forget about trying to become an architect. As little respect as she had for the guy, she had felt sorry for him.

Next to this hung a board that was a total contrast— a complicated slightly messy drawing surrounded by hand-written notes. Carey's project. What a juxtaposition; No wonder Adam had been in such a sour mood out on the lawn. He had probably just looked at the show.

The assignment had been to design public housing, but Carey had designed an entire self-sustaining village. He had argued that low-income housing shouldn't be ghettoized, but rather integrated into the entire town. She peered at one of the notes, remembering his loopy printing.

The hand-drafting and freehand-sketching must look quaint to students now, Iris mused. All drawings, even renderings were done on the computer these days. As she swiveled around to look for one of her own projects, she almost bumped into C.C. standing close enough to breathe on her.

"So, the cops let you go. Or did you tunnel out?"

"I'm out on good behavior."

They eyed each other. Even dressed in baggy shorts and a 'Design will Save the World!' T-shirt, C.C. wore a mantle of authority like a fascist dictator or a gym teacher. All that was missing was a riding crop or whistle. How had she ascended the food chain with so little charm? For the first time, Iris wondered about her background.

"Carey was brilliant, wasn't he?" Iris turned back to Carey's board. "I'll bet he would have accomplished great things if he'd lived."

"He was quite the superstar," C.C. agreed.

Someone jostled Iris on their way to the auditorium, so she stepped out of the circulation path, moving closer to the wall. She tried to picture the hefty C.C. sneaking up behind Carey on a balcony. If the drugs had kicked in by then surprise wouldn't have been required in order to topple him over the edge. Then again, most people braced themselves reflexively when C.C. was around. "So, the house in Lincoln. Are you seriously interested in running it?"

"I am. It's perfect for our September issue. Norman bent my ear about all the green features. Of course he implied that he did most of the design."

"Ri-i-i-ght," Iris said. "I just drafted his ideas. You know, he's dying for this publicity. He thinks it will enhance his swinging bachelor image."

"And you *don't* want it? I toured two alternative projects in Connecticut yesterday afternoon before I flew up here, but I like the Lincoln house best. This could be your lucky break, kid."

Iris noted that C.C. had just alibied herself for the time of Will's killing. "When are you intending to put Norman out of his misery?"

"Oh, I'll tell him before I leave. I just love watching that jerk squirm."

"Can I ask you something? Did you stay in touch with Will or G.B.? You were close with Will at school. Did you talk with him before this reunion?"

"Listen, Nancy Drew, I did not kill Will. I loved his amorality—although I do sympathize with your having had to put up with it. I went to his wedding. Yeah, we stayed friends. He called me last week to say that he'd be here, but we hadn't set up any specific time to meet. I do want to know who knocked him off. As for G.B., I was never one of his favorites. I seem to be lacking in some department. So, is that everything you want to know?"

"Almost. Do you know why Will drugged Carey back at the graduation party?"

"What could that possibly matter at this point, Iris? They're both dead." C.C. stared back at her.

"I just want to know. Why did he do it—the drugging?"

"It was some stupid joke that Will and Adam thought up to get back at Carey for upstaging everyone for all of graduate school."

"Did Alyssa know about it?"

"Who do you think made the brownies? Look it was a joke. That's not what killed him.

"Are you so sure about that?"

For once Iris saw C.C. look uneasy.

CHAPTER 14

Iris trudged back to the jeep. Some joke. They should all be put away for life.

She brightened a bit when she saw that she'd, once again, escaped getting a parking ticket. She called Ellie on her cell phone and filled her in on what she had learned.

Cambridge is notorious for its labyrinth of one-way streets, so from her spot by the Broadway Market—now called something fancier with 'Gourmet' in it—she had to thread her way down Quincy Street, past the Fogg Museum, back into the chaos of Harvard Square.

She punched a radio button for WUMB, the folk music station, and listened to Richard Shindell while she waited for the light to change on Mass Ave. He was singing one of her favorites, his cover of "Cold Missouri Waters." She started singing along as she stared out the window, eyeing the line snaking out of

Bartley's Burgers. She could picture the performer at one of his concerts at Passim's, eyes closed, strumming a relentless guitar beat. This song always choked her up.

A loud honk announced that the light had changed. As she edged up to the next light, a short block further, she looked over at the card tables laden with used books on the sidewalk in front of the Harvard Bookstore. A street person seemed to have set up shop. She wondered what the bookstore thought about their competition. From the corner of her eye she spotted a familiar duck-like gait. Norman! Where was he going and why wasn't he at the panel discussion? Next to him skulked a beige trench-coated figure. Why were Norman and Jerry walking along Mass Ave? She tried to pull into the nearest spot so that she could follow them on foot.

"Miss. You need to move now. That's a handicapped spot!" It was the nasal voice of the same meter maid she'd encountered an hour ago. Damnation.

She pulled back into traffic right as Norman and Jerry disappeared down Holyoke, a one-way street going the wrong direction. She made a left on Dunster, then circled back to Holyoke. They had disappeared. She scanned the block and saw a Thai and a French restaurant. They must have gone into one of those for lunch. A car behind her honked.

All right already! She tried to think fast. What could she do—try to find them and eavesdrop? They were sure to see her. How would she ever explain her presence?

Oh, hell. She jerked the car into drive and headed home, trying to parse out their possible connection.

CHAPTER 15

There were two messages flashing on the phone by the time that Iris got home at one thirty. In the first, Ellie said she had gotten Rachel's cell phone number off their home answering machine. She had tracked her down to her Cambridge hotel and, as one of Will's classmates, offered condolences, asking how she could help. "We set up 'Beep'"—she was cut off.

Next, Luc's message said to call him at the Paradise. She called him.

"Iris, are you okay? Why did the cops haul you off?"

"Because I was supposed to meet with Will yesterday. His wife told the police about it. Luc, I'm worried that someone's trying to set me up for his murder. Ellie and Mack are meeting with me tonight to try to figure out who it could be. Any chance you could join us?"

"Sure, of course. But the cops can't really think that you did it. I can vouch for you being out in Lincoln. Listen, I just got a cancellation for a table tonight, so why don't we meet here at the Paradise at seven? I wanted to thank you and Ellie for the catering gig anyway."

"That would be great—your help and dinner. Thanks. I can't wait to hear your take on these people."

Iris called Ellie next and left a message for them to meet at the Paradise.

By now, it was time for Sheba's walk. She dreaded the thought of seeing where Will's body had been found, but hoped for the chance to still learn something from the raked-over crime scene.

Fresh Pond, four miles west of Iris' house, was an anomaly in Cambridge—300 acres of reservoir and park that Frederick Law Olmsted, the noted landscape architect, had cleverly designed to look undesigned. Iris and Sheba walked the whole 2 ¼ mile dirt-alternating-with-paved path every day.

Someone had come up with the novel idea of driving the nearby nursing home residents around Fresh Pond in bright yellow bicycle-rickshaws. The first time Iris had seen one of these, she'd been sure she was hallucinating. But *the Cambridge Chronicle* that week had shown a clear photo of it with a caption calling it a pedi-cab. They were essentially jogging strollers for those at the other end of the age spectrum. It had been a pedi-cab driver, luckily not one of the frail and excitable 'seniors,' who had spotted the blue of Will's jacket near a path through the woods.

After passing the hazards of the parking lot, Iris unhooked Sheba's leash and the bassett hound trotted into the woods as fast as her short legs would take her. Iris kept up a brisk pace knowing the dog would circle around to keep tabs on her mistress. She relished these daily walks and the snippets of conversation from walkers, joggers, and cyclists that washed over her like sounds from the Tower of Babel.

Two women approached, one with a silk scarf draped over her raincoated shoulders, the other in an olive quilted vest being led by an arrogant-looking black poodle. The dog cast a disdainful look at Sheba who was sniffing an aromatic clump of weed. The second woman rattled away in French "mais les poissons sont si chers chez Le Fishmonger. Moi, je prefere Whole Foods."

This early June day was a rarity for New England weather—neither hot nor cold. As if they had slipped into a chasm between seasons. The scrim of trees ringing the reservoir looked flat against a leaden sky.

Iris heard the approach of the chattering Water Department brigade, power-walking three abreast, cell phones clipped self-importantly to the belts of their pleated chinos. What kind of water-related emergency required a constant tether to the Water Department mothership nestled so close by next to the parking lot? These soldiers weren't the ones doing battle in flooded basements. Ah, yes, terrorists. They must represent Cambridge's first line of defense against anthrax being dribbled into the reservoir. But what were they supposed to do about it—beat the terrorists with their cell phones?

Iris distracted herself with these daydreams about her fellow walkers as she made her way past the dog beach. Sheba sidetracked to take a quick dip and check on which canine friends might be there, then raced to catch up with her.

Up ahead Iris made out the loping gait of the Vietnam vet who always wore a multi-colored fez. She tried to veer out of his line-of-sight but was hemmed in to the right by the reservoir's chain-link fence and to the left by the dog pond. This guy would rant at passers-by on days when he hadn't taken his meds. As she hurried past today, he shouted at her back, "You can't HANDLE the truth!"

Rattled, Iris increased her pace to a jog, but swerved to steer Sheba out of the way of a cyclist hurtling towards them. The rider had a phone mic dangling from under his helmet and was shouting, "everything I'm saying is confidential."

Three quarters of the way around the pond, they came to the path leading up toward the nursing home. She steered a reluctant Sheba onto the unfamiliar trail, which edged alongside 'Butterfly Meadow,' an open marshland that served as a bird sanctuary. Midway up, in a secluded area, broken branches and trampled underbrush ghosted where Will's body must have lain. A remnant of yellow crime scene tape fluttered from a low Sycamore branch. The police had worked quickly. Iris looked down and felt an unalloyed sadness. For the first time Will's death felt real. His life had just vaporized. Had he done anything to make this happen, or was he just in the wrong place at the wrong time?

She slumped down onto the matted leaves and Sheba came over to rest her muzzle in her lap.

Iris needed to think. Somehow Will had gotten here from the airport yesterday, then wound up dead in these woods. Had he arranged to meet someone? Had someone known what flight he was on and surprised him at the airport? No, the airport had cameras everywhere—too risky. Will must have arranged a meeting. But with whom? And why? Lost in thought, she didn't hear the sound of crunching on the path but Sheba started a low growl.

"What are you doing here?" An officious looking man in an olive shirt and pants glared down at her. "You're trespassing on Neville Nursing Home grounds."

"Oh, uh… I knew the man who died here yesterday. I wanted to pay my respects."

"We don't allow trespassers. We have to think of our residents' safety."

"You weren't the one who found him yesterday, were you?"

"Who are you—a reporter?"

"No, I told you, I was a friend of the guy they found here yesterday."

"One of the pedi-cyclists found him."

"Any chance I could talk with him?"

"No, Dave's not here now. You gotta go, lady."

Iris rose wearily to her feet. So much for finding an overlooked clue—a piece of cloth on a branch, a scrap of paper with a phone number… that only happened on TV. She and Sheba trudged back down the hill.

CHAPTER 16

After changing into a sun dress that suggested more than it revealed, Iris threw a sweater over her shoulders and walked the three blocks downhill to the Paradise Café. She surveyed the room for Ellie but didn't see her. Louise, doubling as maitre d' and waitress, seated her at the café's choicest table—now white-draped for the Saturday dinner crowd. It was a few minutes before seven, but the restaurant was already half-filled. Luc had opened this restaurant the previous winter on a corner where restaurants had never managed to succeed before. The combination of his inventive menu, the cheerful interior design, and the sexy owner/chef had hit just the right note. When the restaurant critics started raving about Luc's cooking, it had became impossible for the neighborhood people to get one of the ten coveted tables. The initial buzz had died down a bit, and Iris had settled into the place as her local breakfast canteen. But this was her first time here for dinner.

Evening light from the west-facing windows suffused the taupe walls while the Southern pine floorboards added a caramel glow. This month's display by a local artist consisted of eight oil paintings in fiery tones hung around the two inside walls.

Iris caught the motion of the kitchen door swinging open and Luc strolled out in jeans and a sports jacket, gripping a bottle with the recognizable orange label of Iris' favorite champagne. He spotted her and headed over, his eyes locked on hers. Hair loose, he looked like a Viking Prince. He leaned down and kissed her gently on the lips. The room had become dead quiet.

"How are you holding up?"

Was this what it felt like to swoon? "Um... good. I'm good."

He filled the flutes and toasted, "to your continued liberty." They clinked glasses. "So, catch me up on the latest on this guy Will. Was he actually murdered?" So much for the romantic mood.

"'Fraid so. The police found his body at Fresh Pond where as it happens I'd just been walking my dog."

"Jeez. How did I miss all the blood on your blouse yesterday? In fact, you seemed pretty calm."

"I kill ex-boyfriends all the time. It's gotten routine by now."

"I'll keep that in mind. Actually, most murders are committed by family members. The wife probably did it."

Iris looked at him through her lashes. "What do you mean, most murders—51 percent, 89 percent? How do you know that, anyway?"

"My father used to be a cop—here in Cambridge. I told you I grew up here."

"I knew that, but didn't know about your father. Is he retired now?"

The pulse in Luc's temple fluttered. "He died eight years ago. He was shot by a teenage crack-head."

Iris reached for his hand. "God, I am so sorry. That must have been awful."

Luc's voice turned low. "I had just graduated from culinary school—Johnson & Wales, down in Providence. When that happened, I couldn't deal with it. I took off for Italy and stayed there for seven years. I ended up working in some of the great kitchens of Rome before I got my own place. That was the good part. I finally came back last fall to help take care of my mother. So I went full circle."

Out of the corner of her eye, Iris saw Ellie and Mack enter the restaurant. She silently willed her friends away but they hurried over, gushing with apologies for being late.

First business was ordering Ellie her favorite aperitif, a Lillet. The other three stuck with champagne. Then Luc explained that he was trying out a new chef that night and wanted to taste things without hovering in the kitchen. Louise approached. She was the only post-pubescent female Iris knew who could manage to wear pigtails without looking ridiculous. She recited from memory the short, well-edited menu—three appetizer choices, three entrees, and three desserts. Luc explained that the nine choices varied from day to day depending on the market and his whims. With insider information from him, they ordered their meals. Iris realized that she was starving.

Mack was first to report on what he had learned. "The Medical Examiner on the case turns out to be a woman I knew at med school. She said that they should have the full scoop on Monday, but it looks like the killer tasered Will first, then jabbed him with a needle full of a strong drug, a lethal dose of some kind of muscle relaxer. He died within minutes. The cops haven't found the needle yet."

The table was silent. Iris imagined those agonizing minutes.

"I was able to learn something important this afternoon," Iris wanted to break the spell. "I followed G.B.'s teaching assistant to the auditorium where he complained to G.B. about getting a last-minute call to sub for his Semiotics class on Friday. And get this—the class meets in the early afternoon, just when Will was murdered."

"Wow," Mack said. "That's pretty incriminating. I hope that G.B. didn't spot you eavesdropping."

"I hid up on the balcony. They couldn't see me. But Ellie and I were discussing this and it doesn't necessarily nail G.B. as the killer."

"That's right," Ellie picked up the story. "I sat next to Jerry this afternoon on the bus tour of alumni work. It slipped out that he actually flew up on Thursday and I got the distinct impression that he stayed over at G.B.'s condo in Beacon Hill that night. So, they could have murdered Will together or they could have just been spending the day with each other. Or, for that matter, maybe one of them went his separate way on Friday and met up with Will."

"This is making my head hurt. It seemed so clear this afternoon that G.B. was the killer. Well, at least we know they *could have* done it, separately or together. And speaking of Jerry," Iris said, "after I left the picnic, I saw Jerry and Norman walking together in Harvard Square. I lost them on Holyoke Street, but I think they went into a restaurant for lunch. What could they have had to talk about?"

"He didn't mention that when we talked on the bus. I wonder what he was up to?"

"I can't imagine those two having much in common," Iris said, "but it sure seems as if Jerry's trying to hide his actions. And we know from his brownie comment last night that he knew about Will's drugging Carey. Maybe he was the one who actually killed Carey, and Will didn't say anything about it because he didn't want his own part in the drugging to come out. But maybe after all these years, he got a conscience and decided to rat Jerry out."

"Wait a minute. Back up. What's this 'brownie comment'?" Luc said.

Mack proudly filled Luc in on the clue that he himself had extracted from the previous night's party.

"Oh, and C.C. told me that Alyssa actually made the brownies. So that means Jerry, Alyssa, Adam, C.C. and Will all knew that Carey was going to be in a weakened condition that night," Iris said.

"So out of our suspects, that only leaves G.B. as being in the dark," Mack said, as he passed around a basket of warm bread. "Jerry probably wouldn't have told him beforehand since it was G.B.'s apartment and he could have gotten in trouble if he hadn't stopped it."

Hmmm." Ellie said. "If Jerry was the one who killed Carey, and Will was going to expose him, then he'd have a motive for killing Will, but that could apply to the others as well. We've caught Jerry acting suspicious and furtive, but he always acts that way. I tried last night to get him talking about the graduation party, but he clammed up. He mentioned only that he stayed in Cambridge that summer and worked for G.B. Then he left for Chicago and said that he hadn't kept in touch with anyone but G.B. since then. Of course, he could be lying."

They looked up eagerly as Louise approached with the appetizers. They had ordered plates of fluke ceviche and frizzled clam strips for the table.

"I think I've died and gone to Heaven!" Iris said as she speared a piece of clam.

After every morsel was consumed, Luc excused himself to go compliment the trial chef and make sure that Arnold, his sous-chef, was keeping the pace steady. When he returned, he brought with him a bottle of dry Riesling.

Ellie resumed her report. "On the bus tour, I managed to get Alyssa talking about their ride up on Friday. She complained that they had hit rush-hour traffic on the Mass Pike and barely had time to check in to their hotel to change before getting to the dinner. If she's telling the truth, then that lets them off the hook. That's the kind of thing the police can track down, but how can *we* check what they say?"

Iris nodded. "Same thing with C.C. She said that she was in Connecticut yesterday afternoon checking out two projects for the magazine and flew up here afterward. That could alibi her as well for Will's killing. I guess we'll have to try to get others to verify their stories and to use our knowledge about them to test their credibility."

"Right. We know that every one of them would frame their grandmothers to divert suspicion from themselves. We'll have to hope that they're all too arrogant to consider themselves suspects." Ellie directed her fork toward Iris. "When I spoke with Rachel on the phone, she seemed convinced that you're the one who killed Will. She's sure you lured him east to murder him as revenge for his catting around during graduate school."

"She's forgetting that that was 20 years ago. She gives my memory way too much credit." Still, Iris felt a blush warming her cheeks. She avoided looking at Luc.

"Rachel had overheard Will talking on his cell phone on Wednesday, agreeing to meet someone for lunch before going out to Lincoln. It was someone going to Norman's dinner, judging from Will's side of the conversation. She assumed it was you. She told this to the police and said to check his cell phone call log. I tried to assure Rachel that you didn't do it—that I had talked with you that afternoon. I think I created some doubt in her mind about you being Iris-the-Ripper. She flew out here this morning and is waiting until the ME finishes with the body so she can to take it down to Rhode Island where his family's from."

Luc jumped into the discussion. "Do we know if the police found Will's cell phone? If not, I guess they can trace his records through the phone company. Tracking down that caller sounds like the quickest way to identify the killer."

"But can't people block their number?" Ellie said. "Wouldn't the murderer be sure to do that?"

"Luc, you said that your father was a Cambridge policeman." Mack and Ellie both turned to stare at Iris, then Luc. "Do you know any way we could find out about that call?"

Luc leaned back in his seat. "My father's old partner is still working. We keep in touch. I'll try to see if he'll tell me anything. I think we can assume that they went through the wife's alibi with a fine-toothed comb. The spouse is usually the first person they suspect."

"Unless there's an idiot like me around to catch their eye."

Luc winked at Iris and she felt deliciously happy. She was a suspect in a murder investigation and might even be next on the real murderer's list. But here, in the glow of candlelight, she felt far removed from all that.

There was a moment of quiet appreciation as Louise brought their entrees. Iris had the gnocchi with morel mushrooms and fresh peas. Mac and Ellie had both opted for the scallops with braised fennel, rhubarb beurre blanc, and candied pistachios. Luc rounded out the selections with the rock shrimp in aioli, but the others insisted he taste theirs as well for a proper evaluation of the new chef's try-out.

"This is gastro-porn, my man!" Mack gave Luc a thumbs-up.

The decibel level was starting to climb as the restaurant filled up. "You need more fuzz in here, Luc," Iris said.

He looked at her blankly.

"Fuzz, you know, soft stuff. Curtains, carpet, upholstered chairs. It absorbs the noise."

"Ah, you're right. I'll have to get you in here as a consultant."

The talk segued into a spirited debate about the relative perfection of each dish served that evening with the scallops finally emerging as the evening standout.

That issue resolved, Luc went back to the discussion of murder. "It seems to me that we should try to pin down what each of the five remaining suspects were doing before the dinner. When did you say the police thought he'd been killed, Iris?"

"Between noon and three. That's a good idea, but we'll have to go about it indirectly. Alyssa and Adam claim to have been driving up here during that time frame. Maybe someone saw them pull in to the hotel parking lot. C.C. says that she flew up in the late afternoon. The airline's got to have that on record. then, G.B. and Jerry are the ones that don't seem to have alibis."

"Mack and I are going to the luncheon tomorrow so we can try to pin down what G.B. and Jerry were up to then." Ellie said.

"Yeah, I'm good at finding clues. I'll just put on my dumb-spouse-along-for-the-ride act," Mack said grinning.

"I think I'll talk to Norman," Iris said. "As the reunion chair he might know about people's travel plans. I wish that I could get my hands on the hotel's records showing when people checked in. But I guess the killer could have met with Will beforehand, so that wouldn't really prove anything. Maybe I can pry out of Norman what that lunch with Jerry was about. Somehow I can't see Norman conspiring with Jerry to kill Will. Jerry alone I could see."

"I can pay a visit to my father's partner from the force," Luc volunteered. "Maybe I can pry loose some details about what Malone's got."

Hunched protectively over his rhubarb tart, Mack asked, "Should we tell Detective Malone about anything we've discovered?"

They looked at Luc, their new authority on all things police-related. He shrugged, rubbing a lemon rind around a delicate espresso cup. "It's probably just Jerry's coming up on Thursday and his having lunch with Norman today that they don't know about already. I'll bet they know about G.B. ditching his class. I'm sure they're checking out the alibis of all of the classmates and G.B. You know, our edge isn't just in your knowing the characters involved. It's also the link that you're making between Will's death and Carey's. That may bring up clues that the police aren't focusing on. Once we get more information, that may lead us to motive for both murders. But the police aren't going to believe our interpretation of events, especially if they consider Iris their prime suspect."

Other diners began to stop by the table to compliment Luc on their way out. As the room started to empty, Ellie, Mack, and Iris rose and thanked him for a sublime meal. Before they left, Luc took Iris aside, leaned in to kiss her, and said quietly, "I'm sorry I have to stay to close up. I wish I could walk you home. I said that I'd give the new chef a lift."

"May I take a rain check on that?"

He looked away but smiled, then raised his voice to address all three, "So what's the verdict on the new chef's try-out? Should I hire her?"

CHAPTER 17

Iris sat curled up in her kitchen window seat, reading glasses perched on her nose. She read the clue for 23 across. "Okay, Sheba, four letters that mean 'like some points.' Hmm, 'dots'?"

Sheba opened her mournful eyes to inspect her mistress, then rolled over onto her back—her default reaction when uncertain. But it was nine a.m. on Sunday morning, and that meant the *New York Times* crossword puzzle had Iris' full attention.

Iris squinted at the matrix of letters already filled in and looked off into the distance. She checked her guess against 23 and 24 down, then penned it in. "Ah, 'moot'. They think they're so smart."

She was on her second cappuccino, wondering if it was too early to give Norman a call when the phone rang.

"Sorry to call on a Sunday, Iris. Did everything get sorted out about poor Will?"

"Oh, Norman, I was just going to call you. The police wanted to get me to identify the body, but his wife ended up flying out."

"Surely they don't think that you had anything to do with it," he fished.

"Oh, no. Of course not. Anyway, apart from the police showing up, the Friday night dinner seems to have gone well." She knew this would be how Norman looked at things.

"Yes, I agree. The whole reunion seems to be a success, although we'll still need to tally the funds we've manage to raise. Oh, and you missed it—C.C. was asking questions about the house. I think she may want to feature it in her magazine! But I'm actually calling about something else. I want to take out to Lincoln a few of my best cases of wine and some of the more valuable artwork that I don't want the movers to touch. Can you meet me at the house to help me place some of the paintings? Let's say 2 o'clock—does that work for you?"

"Okay. I guess I can make it. I'll see you there at two."

Iris would be starting a new renovation in Chestnut Hill later in the week and wanted to be done with any loose ends at Norman's house. Frank, the contractor, was halfway through the punch list, and it was going to be hell to get him to pay attention to those last few details now that he had moved on to his next job. This was always the most tedious stage—getting that last two percent of the project done.

Ten minutes later, the phone rang again.

"Mack and I think that you and Luc make a great couple," Ellie began breathlessly.

"Good morning to you too. What's that noise?"

"Disposal. I'm multi-tasking. It looked like we were walking in on something last night."

"Merely an advanced-beginner conversation. I'm following the advice of a friend—moving at glacial speed. Maybe we'll get to second base before I collect social security."

"What is second base anyway? I can't even remember. Said friend is telling you to pick up the pace now. He definitely looks interested and seems like a nice guy. I give you my blessing."

"He does have some interesting miles on him. Do you know that he worked in Italy for seven years and had his own restaurant there? That kind of experience adds more than a decade of sophistication to his age, don't you think? But then again, he's hiring a female chef. She's probably young and gorgeous. They'll be working side by side. He drove her home last night. It's really just a matter of time before they fall in love and he breaks my heart. Do you really want to watch that happen?"

"Oh, she's probably some old crone with a mustache. You'll just have to keep him busy. You said he lived in Italy for seven years? Are we talkin' city or countryside?"

"Rome."

"At least a decade."

"Fine then Madam. For your amusement, I'll throw myself into the fray again. But you may have to pick up the pieces."

"Deal."

CHAPTER 18

"**I** can be subtle, Ellie. Let me tackle Jerry and G.B. I'll do my innocent 'Columbo' bit."

"I know you can, Mack. It's just that they have highly attuned bullshit detectors. If they're the ones who murdered Will and think that we suspect them, we could be the next bodies dumped in the woods. So, be careful. If you can get them talking in some casual way, great. Otherwise, make small talk and wander off. I'll do the same with Adam, Alyssa and C.C."

The car lock chirped and they set out toward GSD for the Sunday luncheon finale. The hum of activity drew them through the lobby back to the first-floor lunch room which had been set up with a buffet so alums and professors could mill around or perch on chairs with plates teetering on their laps while they chatted. Roger Barton, Norman's reunion co-chair, appeared to have finished or given up making any more official pitches.

After loading up his plate with mysterious pasta salads, Mack ambled toward G.B. and Jerry, sitting at a table by themselves.

Ellie overheard him say, "May I join you? We didn't get much chance to talk Friday night. G.B., I've heard so much about your theory classes from my wife."

They looked taken back by this boldness. A piece of potato salad fell off of Jerry's fork as he stared. But appealing to G.B.'s vanity was a wise move. The professor's chest seemed to puff up.

Good, Ellie thought. Mack's foot is in the figurative door.

"Ellie may have ended up writing about architecture rather than practicing it, but I'd love to hear how you both go through the process of designing buildings. Do you really sketch on napkins?"

Brother. Mack was laying it on thick. But G.B. and Jerry seemed to loosen up, and five minutes later, Ellie was amazed to see the three of them engaged in a lively discussion. Meanwhile, she had parked herself near Alyssa and was waiting for her to finish sucking up to their former architectural history professor. She couldn't see any of the other suspects.

"Professor Bachman, I kept hearing your words about the Minoans the entire time we wandered around Knossos."

When the professor was finally rescued by other alums, Ellie swooped in.

"Hey Alyssa. Last day of the reunion—how do you think it's gone?"

"Well," she sighed dramatically. "I have to admit I'm disappointed. No one from our group was at the dinner dance last night. It was filled with all these background people that I didn't even know. They were probably from Landscape or Urban Design. And Will's death on Friday put such a damper on everything." She looked as if she might stamp her foot and shake her curls at this rude disruption of her plans. "Do you know if they've found out yet who did it?"

"I haven't heard of a suspect, but I think that the police have pretty much eliminated Iris."

"But don't they have any ideas about who it could have been?"

"None yet that I know of. Where are C.C. and Adam?"

"She checked out this morning—said that she couldn't wait to get back to the safe haven of Manhattan. Adam's off playing squash with Arturo Herrera." Alyssa consulted her Cartier tank watch. "He'd better get back soon so we can pack up the Bimmer. I don't want to get stuck in weekend traffic again. Now where did I just see G.B.?"

They turned in unison and spotted Mack, off in a corner, still talking animatedly with G.B. and Jerry. As the women approached, they heard Mack explaining "... kind of muscle relaxer. It would have taken several minutes to actually kill him. It depends on a lot of factors."

Unbelievable! Mack had gone off-message and *they* were pumping *him* for information. Ellie put on her pleasant face, silently cursing as Alyssa buttonholed G.B., leading him off to a more private location. Then she turned to Mack. "Would you get me more of that delicious quiche, dear?"

Mack snapped a look at her, then headed back to the food line. Ellie hated quiche.

"So, Jerry, did you and Norman have a nice lunch yesterday? You didn't mention it on our bus ride."

"Wha—why yes, we had a nice chance to catch up. We didn't have much opportunity to talk on Friday night." Jerry had made a quick recovery, pasting a sphinx-like smile on his face and staring off through the room's rear window wall to the GSD's pocket-sized backyard. Ellie could practically hear the wheels spinning in Jerry's brain. She weighed her options, then plunged ahead.

"Last night's dinner got overshadowed by news of Will's death. I'm curious about something you said after learning that the police had found him. You said it was Carey's payback for Will giving him a drugged brownie at the graduation party."

Jerry looked at her sharply. Ellie knew she had abandoned caution—just what she'd told Mack not to do. This was dangerous. But her friend was being set up as a murderer. And one of them had pushed Carey off the balcony. She was determined to shake loose some information of value and figured that, even if Jerry was the killer, he couldn't do much to her in a public place.

He studied her face to gauge how much she knew. "Oh, I was just making a tasteless joke. I didn't mean anything by it. *Obviously* Carey's ghost didn't return to avenge him."

"No, no, I think you may be onto something. We all know by now that Will drugged Carey at the party."

She leaned closer in a conspiratorial pose. "Do you think that Will might have followed Carey into the bedroom and pushed him off the balcony?"

Jerry's rigid stance relaxed an iota. He plucked at an imaginary piece of lint on his beige sports jacket. "No, Will didn't follow him."

"How can you be so sure?"

"Because I saw Will go into the bathroom with Sharon Abramson. They only came out when people near the window started screaming."

"Aaah. That sounds like Will. I was just wondering if there could be any connection between Carey's death and Will's, but it sounds like there wasn't one. Boy, you sure have a good memory, Jerry."

As Mack returned holding a paper plate of quiche, Ellie said, "Honey, we've got to go relieve the babysitter. Bye, Jerry," She knew he would never remember that their daughter was now college-aged.

CHAPTER 19

Iris spotted the gray Prius by the front door in *her* usual spot. The house was no longer a building site, so now she was relegated to "visitor" parking. As she approached the entry, the dramatic pathos of Mozart's *Don Giovanni* blasted out from the open front door. Pressing hands over ears, she raced to the living room and twisted the control knob on the sound system.

"Norman? Where are you?" The house reverberated with silence. She could see several wrapped parcels abandoned on the living room hearth, but no sign of the house's owner. If he were down in the wine cellar he'd be deaf to her cries.

A sound—smack— came from below. Was that a door slamming? What was going on? Norman had dragged her out here on a Sunday to help him and now he was wasting her time. As she marched down two flights of stairs to give him a piece of her mind she heard a rumbling noise, but it seemed to come from outside. Probably a neighbor's lawnmower. She paused before the closed wine cellar door. No doubt Norman was sitting in there mesmerized, sorting through his beloved La Taches and Chateau d'Yquems. She popped open the panel with her closed fist. It was pitch black. She groped for the light switch.

Norman stared back at her, his contorted face pressed up against the inside glass of the wine refrigerator, his body hunched in a fetal position. Saliva escaped from the side of his mouth, and his leaden eyes looked right through her.

Iris let out a primal, blood-curdling scream which devolved into shallow gasps. She tried to look away but couldn't. Backing up until she felt the cool wall behind her, she wrapped her arms around her and took deep breaths.

Maybe he wasn't dead yet. Should she call for help? Get him out of there? Do CPR? Then another thought intruded: whoever put Norman in there might still be in this room hiding, watching her. Her eyes darted around, but her body felt frozen. Hadn't she heard a door slam?

As she stood glued to the wall, noticing the refrigerator shelves thrown on the floor, she heard heavy footsteps thumping down the stairs. He was coming back! A weapon. She needed a weapon. She grabbed a heavy brass candlestick from the table and slid behind the door. The steps got closer. She raised her arm ready to strike.

A sharp intake of a man's breath caught her in time to allow her to divert her makeshift club past his head to crash on the floor. Frank stood framed in the doorway with his arms held up around his ears. "What the hell..." he howled. His voice trailed off as he spotted Norman's entombed body.

"What are you doing here?" she screeched.

"Oh my god. Who killed him—you?" he asked, eyes wild.

"Of course *I* didn't! I was the one who screamed."

They both stood their ground until Frank moved toward the wine cooler. Iris slipped out behind him and scrambled up the stairs to the kitchen. She hunted for her cell in the bottom of her purse and scrolled down for Detective Malone's number. As she reported what she'd found she heard Frank out in the hall talking to the 911 operator.

She put her head between her knees and counted to ten. After a few minutes, her heart's jackhammering began to slacken. She looked up to see Frank in the doorway, observing her.

"*I'm* here 'cause the new trees have to be watered every day. I heard you scream. Why are *you* here?"

"Norman asked me to help him place some artwork."

They eyed each other suspiciously then perched at opposite ends of the kitchen table, not speaking, until they heard the sound of cars kicking up stones on the driveway. They both made their way to the front door and saw a Crown Vic and a Lincoln Police vehicle, blue gumball strobing, skid to adjacent stops. The Lincoln uniformed officers conferred with Detectives Malone and Connors, then all four strode in.

"Ms. Reid. It seems that you are not having a good week-end," Malone said.

"I've had better. Norman Meeker's body is two flights down in the wine cellar."

CHAPTER 20

"May I please speak with my client privately?" Stirling asked in an aggrieved voice. Detective Malone left them in an interview room, the harsh fluorescent lighting making Iris' headache throb.

"What the hell do you think you're doing, Iris? This is not my idea of lying low! I tell you to stay out of trouble and two days later, you're found with another dead classmate! Are you insane?" His tone suggested that Iris was mischievously courting corpses merely to annoy him.

She stood facing him with her arms folded. "I'm sorry to have to call you off the golf course on a Sunday, Stirling. If you are having trouble seeing me as innocent until proven guilty, I can always switch lawyers and get someone from Shaw, Huntington and Barrett. They'll probably give me the benefit of the doubt for being in the wrong places at the wrong times."

"Is that all this is supposed to be—a series of coincidences? And how is it supposed to make me look if you go to our competitors to represent you? Everyone knows you're my sister."

"I don't really care how this reflects on you. This is not about *you!*"

They held each other in a death-stare for a full minute.

"Cut me some slack, Stirling, okay? I've just come face to face with the corpse of my murdered client who two hours ago summoned me to meet with him. I'm either the next victim or being framed by the murderer. If all you can focus on is that your reputation might be tarnished by association with a sister who's involved in a murder investigation, then I'll get another lawyer. Here's my question. Can you represent me as if I were one of your regular clients?"

"Fine, fine. Let's calm down, okay? I think you need me as your lawyer right now. Just tell me what happened."

Iris closed her eyes and shook her head. She wanted to float back to her feeling of safety from the previous night. "You can hear it when they take my statement."

An hour later as they left the police station, Stirling said "I can't believe that out of your GSD class of what—sixty students?—there have been two people murdered."

"Three," Iris corrected.

CHAPTER 21

"Pum… pum." A basketball pounded rhythmically against a neighboring garage backboard. Luc approached Ed's weathered triple-decker, noticing the brown paint peeling from the clapboards. He should ask the guys down at the precinct for the name of a good painter. A breeze wafted a candy smell from an overgrown viburnum bush that had stood sentinel at this porch for as long as Luc could remember. Only the sweating six-pack cradled in his arm separated him from the kid who once waited here with his father.

"Well, look who the cat dragged in." Ed must have been sitting in his usual ratty living room chair, several feet inside. "You still wearing girl hair?" he teased as he gave Luc an affectionate bear hug. Ed was a bear himself—six feet of bulk that barely complied with police fitness regulations.

"You sound just like Pop. You know I need to pull it back when I'm cooking so it doesn't get in the food. Give me a break." Luc held up the Narragansett beer he'd brought. "Want some company for the game?"

On a summer Sunday afternoon in Massachusetts, there's never any question about which game. It's always the Red Sox.

"So, how's your mother?" Ed asked as he resumed his spot facing the TV. Luc sank into the plaid companion chair and snapped open a beer, passing it to Ed.

When Ed had lost his wife to cancer three years earlier, Luc and his sister had urged their mother to give Ed a call—maybe invite him over for a meal. But she had resisted all efforts to get her to socialize. By then, she had even given up on the church. God was supposed to have protected her husband. That was the deal she had made in all those masses. Without her daily church visits, she'd lost most of her links to the outside world.

"She's the same—won't go out. She watches her soaps and waits for visits with the grandkids. Now that I'm back, I've joined the campaign to try to get her interested in something. I did get her down to the restaurant last week."

Ed noticed the time on the plastic clock atop the TV. "Hey. Game's on!" He fiddled with the remote and the image of the shaved-headed Masterson and Pedroia, hats over hearts, appeared as the national anthem was warbled by a soprano in the background.

"This game had better get the Sox back on top," Ed muttered. "Tampa's kept our seat warm long enough. The guys don't need Papi to step it up against the Rays."

The crowd repeated the sing-songy "Let's go, Red Sox," clap, clap, clap. The earlier drizzle had let up and the sky had cleared. After the preliminary practice swings and throws were out of the way, the game began.

"Let's hope Drew, Manny and Lowell can keep the big bats going. Are Pena and Ortiz still on the disabled list?" Luc asked.

"Yup. Ortiz is out for a couple more weeks." They watched in silence until Ed erupted at the screen, "Oh, Beckett! Don't you get it? You're not supposed to give up any hits! Just get out of this inning and settle down. Hit the corners, Josh. Pitch from ahead and stop giving up line drives."

Luc's lips curved up at one corner. Ed had been his little-league coach. He remembered how emotional the guy could get about the game.

After another ten minutes of snorts and groans, Ed looked over and said, "By the way, did you sign those divorce papers yet?"

Luc's jaw muscle spasmed. He stared intently at the TV while flipping the top back from a beer. His sister had a big mouth. "I'm working on it. Look at that— Beckett left that curve way high and Upton still couldn't handle it."

Ed said quietly "It's time to get on with your life, kid."

The teams exchanged places on the field a few times. The Sox were ahead 5-4. Third baseman, Mikey Lowell, came up to bat. The ball sailed toward the second row Green Monster seats and the crowd roared. The ump flung out his left arm. The crowd erupted with fury.

"Unbelievable!" Luc turned to Ed. "Did you see that? That was a clear 4-bagger. Look—here's the replay. Am I right?" They watched NESN's freeze-frame.

"Screw you, Remy. Goddamn umpires."

" Doesn't NESN have another camera behind home plate showing left field?"

"The Sox get screwed at least once a game on home run calls. What is it—retribution for the umps getting Bellhorn's home run correct?"

"Don't worry. Manny will make things right again."

"Hey, Dusty's walking!"

" Magadan's going to have a stern talk with Pedroia when he gets back to the dugout."

"When are you coming back to eat at the restaurant? You haven't been in since the opening party."

"You know I'm not so good with eating out on my own."

"I'll eat with you. Maybe I'll invite this new friend of mine to join us."

"As in new female friend?" Ed cocked an eyebrow.

Luc used this entree to bring up the subject he had come to talk about.

CHAPTER 22

Shocked, Ellie's hand flew to her mouth. "No," she whispered. "Norman's been murdered—and you found his body?" She wrapped her arms around her friend as they stood on her kitchen stoop. "You're trembling. Come in and let me get you something to drink."

"His eyes seemed to be staring at me and his face was mushed up against the glass door. I'm never going to be able to get that image out of my head."

Ellie rubbed Iris' back. "Sit down and I'll make you tea and cinnamon toast. Or do you want something stronger? Hootch? It's five o'clock—almost cocktail hour."

Iris had been drawn straight from the police station to Ellie's house, knowing she would find comfort here.

Her shoulders began to loosen. "Tea's perfect— the British empire's cure for any crisis."

The smell of cinnamon soon suffused the cozy kitchen. Ellie poured more Earl Grey into Iris' mug. "Three murders! This has gotten too dangerous, Iris. We should leave it to the police now. We seem to be at a dead end anyway." She covered her mouth. "I can't believe I said that. At least they can't pin Norman's murder on you. You're the one who called Detective Malone."

"They could think I did that to throw them off track. Frank showed up after I found the body, but he can't vouch for me that I didn't stash it there first, then act like a terrified innocent."

"Frank, the contractor? What was he doing there? Could he have killed Norman?"

"I doubt it. He said that he was there to water some newly planted trees. That's credible. Besides, if he had done it, he wouldn't have stuck around to respond to my scream."

"Okay, scratch him. But we need to figure this out. We should be safe enough with our sleuthing inside this kitchen. I wonder if Norman was injected with the same drug as Will? The two killings have got to be related."

"Maybe Mack can get that information from his ME buddy."

"Speaking of my master-sleuth husband, we went to the final reunion luncheon today. Mack's assignment was to chat up G.B. and Jerry. He was supposed to be subtle about it, but when I joined them, I found *them* pumping *Mack* for information about the drug that Will's killer had used."

"Sounds like morbid curiosity—right up their alley. But if they were the killers, they would know what they had used. Plus, if they were at the luncheon, they couldn't have been out in Lincoln killing poor Norman. Unless they hired a hit man. Norman called me at noon and I found him soon after two. Didn't we narrow down the suspect list for Will's killer to Jerry and/or G.B.? But now it looks like you're their alibi for Norman's murder. Who else from our suspect list was at the luncheon?"

"Alyssa told me that C.C. flew back to New York Sunday morning. But that doesn't mean that she didn't nip out to Lincoln on her way to the airport to bump off Norman."

"Maybe. But she seems to have that alibi for Friday. Was Adam there?"

"Alyssa said that he was playing squash with Arturo Herrera. That should be easy enough to check. Oh, and I was able to pry Jerry loose from G.B. long enough to unearth an alibi for Will and himself during the critical time at the graduation party."

"Is it a credible alibi? I can just picture that weasel taking advantage of Carey's having been out-of-it."

"His alibi is that he had his eyes pinned to Will's every movement during the party. I get the sense that he had the hots for your boyfriend back then. Who knew?"

"Well, that's one person at least that Will never slept with. At least I don't think ..."

Changing the subject fast, Ellie gabbed a pad of paper from her nearby desk and said "Let's make a matrix of the five suspects' actions during the three murders. This is getting way too complicated to keep in our heads."

They eliminated Will from the suspect list, so that left: G.B., Adam, Alyssa or C.C. as suspects in Carey's death; G.B. or Jerry as suspects in Will's death, and only Adam or C.C. as suspects in Norman's death.

"So, no one person could have killed all three?" Ellie said.

Iris frowned at their chart. "That's what our chart says."

"There have been three murders and we still don't have all the pieces," Ellie started to clear the dishes from the table. "I think we'll have to let the police take it from here—examine fibers or get DNA evidence— whatever they do to get proof. This may be as far as we can get by shaking the trees."

"Still, I think we're getting closer. But it's too dangerous for us to poke around anymore. Besides, Detective Malone said he'd charge me with obstruction of justice if I turned up at any more murder scenes."

"Well, that's not fair. The murderer is setting you up."

"We know that, but the police don't. Still, I can't stand the thought of the murderer slipping away again like he or she did 20 years ago. Norman didn't deserve to die. He was irritating, sure. He could get jammed on 'play,' but he was basically a harmless, if pretentious, nerd."

"I think it's time for us to keep our distance from all the people at that dinner." Ellie said as she wiped a butter knife with a paper towel. "But we also need to keep the police from thinking you're the killer. You did have strong connections to all three victims. What is your brother doing to defend you?"

"He's telling me to avoid providing any more damning circumstantial evidence, or I'll get sent to the chair."

"Swell. The police need to get this wrapped up soon, before someone else gets killed. They need to get somebody behind bars. And we need to insulate ourselves from the whole thing. Tomorrow I'll get back to the second draft of my book and you'll start your new project in Chestnut Hill. Then Raven gets back from RISD on Wednesday. You promised to make her a cake. Meanwhile, we'll leave this for the police to figure out. Agreed?"

"Absolutely," Iris crossed her heart and had every intention of sticking to this plan.

CHAPTER 23

She was startled to hear her doorbell ring at dinnertime that evening. Few people except Sierra Club solicitors ever approached her front door. She saw Luc through the door's glass panel, his blue eyes twinkling. Sheba looked up at her quizzically.

"You order a pizza, ma'am?" He held up a large box from Emma's—the source of the best gourmet pizza in Cambridge.

She gave him a grin, chin raised. "Depends. What's on it?"

He peeked into the box: "Chevre and basil?" He cocked an eyebrow. Iris had always wanted to be able to do that. As a girl she used to practice isolating just one brow while she sat with her mother in church, but she'd never succeeded.

"Yup. That's mine. Come on in, young man."

He handed her a padded yellow envelope.

"What's this?"

"I don't know. It was sticking out of your mail slot." He bent to pat Sheba, who was sniffing intently at the box. The aroma was tantalizing.

"Watch out. That's my vicious watch dog Sheba."

At hearing her name, Sheba rolled onto her back, legs in air.

"Vicious." Luc laughed. "I can see that." He obliged the watch dog with a full-belly rub.

As she led him back to the kitchen, Iris turned down Lucinda Williams' languid, bad-girl voice crooning "Words Fell", and tossed the envelope on the kitchen's island.

"Don't turn down Lucinda on my account," he said.

"Actually, I've been trying to drown out what happened this afternoon."

"What else could've possibly happened?" He set down the box on the kitchen table and looked at her, turning serious.

"I know, it's incredible but there's been another death. Norman. I found his body out in Lincoln." She rested the palms of her hands on her eyes.

Luc erupted into coughing before he managed to wheeze out "wha-a-at? Norman's dead? We just saw the guy. Was it an accident? Are you okay?"—all interspersed with more coughing.

"Do you want some water? How about a beer?" She hurried to get two bottles of Sam Adams and a bottle opener.

"No, it looks like murder again, using the same method as with Will. Norman called this morning. God, it was just this morning! He asked me to come out there to help him hang some artwork. When I got there, I couldn't find him. I thought he might be down in the wine cellar and couldn't hear me. Well, he *was* down there. Someone had stuffed his dead body into the wine refrigerator."

He stared at her, open-mouthed. Then, he snapped his mouth closed and said, "Damn."

She looked down and studied the pizza. She couldn't get the ugly image of Norman's corpse out of her head.

"Iris, why don't you move in with Ellie for awhile—just until the killer is found? You could be next on this guy's list. There's a psycho running around and now two people are dead—no, three."

"I know. I will lie low. But the people from the reunion have all left by now except G.B., and I never run into him. I intend to leave all further sleuthing to the police. I just hope they can manage to figure out who's doing this. I have no sense of whether they're getting anywhere. Detective Malone is playing his cards close to the vest."

Luc hesitated. "I don't know if I should even mention this now, but I saw my father's old partner this afternoon. We talked and I tried to get out of him anything he might have heard about the case. At first Ed didn't want to say anything at all, but then he loosened up. He says they haven't found Will's cell phone yet and the wife's alibi checks out. Also, C.C., Alyssa and Adam are in the clear for the time frame of Will's death. That's all he knows. Or all he'd tell me. I did ask him if he remembered that case from 20 years ago, of the Harvard student going off the balcony, and he did. They thought it was a clear-cut drug thing, tragic but all too common. Then he went on to say that one thing had always bothered him about the case. The kid's apartment had been tossed before they got there the next day—you know, burglarized. It's sometimes hard to tell the difference between the usual mess of a student's apartment, especially at the end of a term, and a place that's been systematically searched, but he had the definite impression that it had been gone through."

"Hmmm. I wonder if Carey's friend, Patty, knows anything about that. Would it be dangerous to talk with her?"

"Please Iris, don't risk it."

Luc, then Iris, picked up a pizza slice, now cold, and chewed in preoccupied silence.

"This is amazing pizza. I'm sorry I'm not better company tonight."

"I'd say discovering a corpse a few hours ago is a good excuse for not feeling chatty. Would you like me to go?"

"No, I'm glad you're here but I've completely lost my appetite and this pizza is too good to waste."

"Here, I'll wrap it up. You can have it tomorrow."

Luc crushed the pizza box into her recycling bin by the back door while Iris cleared the plates. She glanced at the envelope still on the counter. No address or name. As she tore open the flap, her mind had a split second to register the scraping sound.

CHAPTER 24

"Ooooh, God. My head is in a vise," Iris moaned.

The next thing she blurted out, after she opened her eyes and registered the hospital bed she lay in, was "Don't call my brother!"

Detective Malone couldn't hold back a snort of laughter.

She smelled something burning. The explosion came back to her. "Where's Luc? Is he okay?"

"Right here. I'm fine," he said, leaning forward in a chair next to her bed, his face filled with concern. The dim light coming through the window behind him hinted at some time in the evening.

"Do you want me to get the nurse for more pain meds?" luc asked.

Her head throbbed, but she wanted to get answers before losing her concentration.

"That's okay. I'll wait. What about Sheba? Did she get hurt?"

"No, no, she's fine. When the ambulance came, your neighbor, the woman with the gray braid, came over to see what happened. She said that Sheba could stay with her—said she looks after her sometimes when you're away."

"Right, that's good. What happened? There was an explosion, wasn't there?"

Detective Malone leaned against the door, watching her. "You got a letter bomb. It was a crude device—match-heads on one side of the flap and flint on the other. When you tore it, the burst of flames knocked you back and you hit your head on the edge of the counter. This could have killed you instead of just leaving you with minor burns. Your friend here thought fast, put out the fire, and called 911. We couldn't find any prints on the remains of the envelope. The doctors are keeping you here overnight to watch your burn blisters and make sure you don't have a concussion."

Iris felt the edges of a bandage on the side of her forehead. That's what was throbbing, she realized. She could see another bandage extending up her neck from under the hospital johnny. "Did it burn my face?"

"No," the detective said. "I'm told that your friend here smothered the flames before they could do much damage."

She looked across at Luc and smiled weakly. "Good work, bodyguard. Thank God you were there. A letter bomb—I can't believe it!"

"I know, it's crazy. I called Ellie and she's on her way. She's bringing some of your things," Luc said, reaching for her hand and giving it a squeeze.

"I don't mean to interrupt, Ms. Reid, but I'd like to go over anything you might remember that could have triggered this attempt on your life."

"That's just it. I can't make any sense out of the last few days. You know how I spent most of today, Detective. I've told you everything I know about Will and Norman. I can't figure out any connection between them, and yet there must be one. What can *you* tell *me* about what's going on?"

"I can't talk about the murder investigations, but I can say that my detectives are canvassing your neighborhood to see if anyone saw who dropped off this envelope. This murderer is clever and he's getting bolder. Still, his luck can't go on like this forever. Someone's going to spot something out of place. What concerns me is your safety. You're lucky to be alive. He, or she for that matter, seems to think you know something that might incriminate him."

"All I know is that Will's wife told Ellie she overheard him talking on his cell saying he would meet someone for lunch on Friday and then drive out with them to the dinner later on."

"Yes, we got that information too. We've been checking out everyone at the Friday night dinner and their alibis. But Ms. Reid, I can't stress this enough, this bomb was meant to silence you. Let us do the investigating. If anything occurs to you, any connections from the past that you see in a different light, call me immediately. Don't try to follow up on anything yourself. It's gotten too dangerous. You have my number."

"I have it and I'll call you, I promise."

As Detective Malone walked out, a nurse in hippo-patterned scrubs strode in brandishing a blood pressure cuff. "Time to check your vitals," she called out cheerfully.

Luc stood up and squeezed her gently on the shoulder. "I should take off. I'll call you in the morning. I hope you can sleep in here."

"Don't worry. I'll get them to give me some good drugs. Thanks again for helping me."

He smiled back at her, then walked out.

"That your boyfriend? He seems nice," the nurse said while pumping the cuff excruciatingly tight.

"If I'm lucky," Iris said staring at the hippos. Had this nurse strayed from the pediatrics ward?

Iris' vitals noted, the nurse swept out just as Ellie entered. "Great hairdo, darlin'. It looks like something Raven might have created." She gently gave Iris a kiss on the forehead. "Poor baby."

"How bad do I look? I smell like an incinerator."

"Don't worry. I brought my hair-cutting shears. We'll just give you some layers in the front."

CHAPTER 25

"I look like Karen Carpenter!" Iris moaned as she inspected herself in the hospital's bathroom mirror. "Do you think I'll bring back the 'shag'?"

"Now don't you be dissin your hairdresser, girl."

"I'm sorry. I'm such an ungrateful wretch. Thank you for salvaging what you could. Can you believe someone sent me a letter bomb? It's not that I was hoping to win Miss Congeniality, but it's hard not to take this personally." She slid back into the bed and her head started to throb again.

"Someone thinks you know something."

"Maybe I do have some vital clue buried deep in my sub-conscious. I think I need a hypnotist." Iris pried off an edge of the gauze bandage and peered at the burns on her upper chest. Even through the white salve coating her skin, she could see the ugly red blisters.

"I guess I won't be showing a lot of cleavage for awhile."

"How does it feel? Do they itch?"

"Not too bad yet. They'll probably itch when they dry out."

"Luc said that Detective Malone was here. Who does he think is behind all this?"

"He said that the murderer hasn't made any mistakes yet, but that sooner or later he or she would slip up."

"Well, doesn't that inspire confidence. We could all be butchered in our beds by then. Where's Chief Inspector Jane Tennison when you need her?"

"The police said that Norman's body was still slightly warm, despite the wine refrigerator being on, so he must have been killed either right before I drove up or while I was upstairs."

"Ugh! What a creepy thought. But wouldn't you have heard something or seen a car if it had happened while you were there?"

"I saw Norman's Prius in the upper driveway, but the murderer could have parked in the garage on the side. I wouldn't have seen it when I came to the front door. There was loud music on when I got there, so it was hard to hear anything. Since the garage is on the middle level between the wine cellar and main floor above, the murderer could have escaped through the garage while I was up in the kitchen. Come to think of it, I think I did hear a door slam."

"Did you tell that to Detective Malone?"

"All except the door slamming. I just remembered that."

"You should tell him."

"He'll probably think I'm trying to divert suspicion from myself again."

"Oh, come on. The police can't possibly think that you killed Norman and stuffed him in the wine refrigerator. Think of all the valuable wine that might have gotten wrecked. You'd never do that!"

"Very funny. True as well. Why didn't I think of using the wine snob defense?"

"So our timeline doesn't show us anyone who could have killed both Will and Norman. Unless you actually *did* do it, Iris."

"With my middle-age memory, I wouldn't rule me out."

CHAPTER 26

O n Monday morning, as soon as she could convince her doctor to release her, she walked from Mt. Auburn Hospital to one of her favorite places in Cambridge, Formaggio Kitchen, a gourmet deli. Aside from being packed to the rafters with unusual food, its floor plan of three rooms laid out in a row had always intrigued her. Iris grabbed a basket and headed toward the cheese case. She studied the different choices. Stinky epoisses sat haunch-to-haunch with raw-milk chevre, mimolettes, brebis, and a huge wheel of gruyere—many of them aged in the shop's own basement 'cave.' She lingered over two choices, discussing their merits with the salesperson, a skinny young man with an eager expression. After settling on a wedge of pecorino, she moved on to the cured meats that shared the glass-fronted display. She debated among the prepared foods, pates, exotic condiments, and the expensive but well edited wine selection.

With her basket half filled, she moved on to the store's middle room, a 'captive room', accessed only through one of the other two. This tiny jewel box was filled with all things sweet. Pastel petit-fours, madeleines dipped in chocolate and a dozen different kinds of cakes and cookies were on display. But Iris delighted most in the exotic brightly-wrapped candies lining the floor-to-ceiling shelves—hand-cut sherbet-colored marshmallows, green apple lollipops, and sugary fondants. This room was straight out of her childhood fantasies. She hesitated, then had two fruit tarts carefully wrapped in a bakery box.

The last room was the largest. It was an elegant grocery with the platonic ideal of each category on offer. One could find perfectly ripe organic mission figs or tart bilberry nectar. Along the edges of the minuscule aisles could be found fresh brioches, burnt caramel ice cream, or eggplants so beautiful they might have been sculpted from wax. There was even a flower shop within the grocery space offering exquisite single blooms at impressive prices. She considered getting some flowers, but didn't want to overdo her thank-you picnic for Luc and run the risk of embarrassing him.

It was just after noon by the time she returned home and it dawned on her that Luc might be overseeing the lunch shift at the café. She had never actually been at the Paradise during lunchtime, and realized she didn't know his schedule. She had imagined the two of them enjoying this picnic in his apartment. She searched on line to find his home phone number and noticed that he lived on Arlington Street—Ellie's street. She was surprised that they hadn't ever bumped into him walking around the neighborhood. His building was on the odd side, not the even. Good. That meant that it wasn't the condo building with the ugly modern entryways.

"Hello?" His voice sounded ragged, tentative.

"Oh, God. I've woken you up. It's Iris. Go back to sleep—sorry…"

"No, that's okay. I need to get up soon anyway. I'm up early to visit the markets, and help with the breakfast crowd, then come home to get a few more hours of sleep before starting the dinner prep. I usually wake up around now. It's good to hear from you. How's the head feeling? Are you home now?"

"There's no pain that Advil can't handle at this point. I'm home, and I wanted to drop by with something for you."

"Great. Come on over. Do you know where I am? It's the corner of Mass Ave and Arlington Street, above the Paper Source—Building 3, third floor, door on the right. I can buzz you in. Just give me fifteen minutes to take a shower."

CHAPTER 27

This was always the tricky part for Iris. Being so visually particular, she had a hard time being with someone with bad taste. What if Luc's living room featured a clunky pleather sofa with floral wing chairs facing an enormous TV? More than one of her relationships had been scuttled when the guy's place had spaghetti sauce encrusted on the stove's burners or toothpaste spit on the medicine chest. But then Luc had designed the interior of the Paradise Café, and that was tasteful.

She got buzzed into a well-maintained lobby with an old-fashioned cage-type elevator. As she got out on the third floor, she heard a blues riff that she didn't recognize seeping out from an open door.

"Luc?"

He came into his foyer wearing jeans and a white button-down shirt, drying his hair with a towel. His skin looked rosy from the warm shower. The open top buttons of his shirt revealed light brown chest hair. He looked vulnerable and sexy. Before she could think about it, she kissed him on the lips and felt his responding warmth. The same scent from their kiss in the café reached her—spicy and a little woodsy. Was it aftershave or an exotic Italian soap that he'd gotten in Rome?

"Iris," he said.

"Hi," she said softly. He would probably think she was a desperate cougar if she jumped him now. She winced, turned away, but was then drawn into an airy, inviting living room beyond. It had high ceilings, enormous windows and deep crown moldings. The furniture, however, was sleek and modern. Iris had always liked that juxtaposition of modern furnishings in a classic setting. But more impressive was the room's balance between order and relaxation. She wandered over to an ornate wooden fireplace mantle flanked by floor-to-ceiling bookcases. On the shelves personal things—photographs and mementos, were interspersed with over a hundred books. Magazines and newspapers were piled on a coffee table alongside a pottery plate that read *Capri*. Luc watched her curiously.

"This place looks so European. I love it," she said.

"That's why I bought it—the architecture reminds me of my place in Rome. You can't believe how many boring, generic condos there are out there. Let me help you with these bags. What have you brought?"

"It's some lunch things to thank you for being my good Samaritan last night."

"*Di niente.*" He bowed slightly. "All part of my job as bodyguard."

She followed him into a large corner room where sunlight bathed the cream-colored walls. A formidable Aga range held court against a back wall of restaurant-grade appliances.

"This is the main reason I bought the place—the serious kitchen. But I never get a chance to use it with all the time I spend at the café." He rested the bags on the marble counter. "Are these from Formaggio? I love that place!"

Iris relaxed at an ancient pine table, smiling as she watched Luc lift items out of the bags like a boy at Christmas. "Aah, real pecorino!" He held it up to his nose, inhaled deeply, and sighed. Then holding up the wine bottle to read the label he exclaimed, " I didn't know they exported this! You are transporting me back to Italia, *cara*."

"And you don't even have to cook." She liked that he had called her *'cara'*.

"You have to taste this wine—a 2005 Tenuta Migliardonico 'Chateau de Novi' Gavi!" The 'r' rolled off his tongue convincingly. He opened the bottle and filled two glasses. "Did you know that the Castello Gavi was once used as Napoleon's headquarters?"

"Being French, I'll bet he located his fortresses on the basis of the quality of the nearby vineyards." She took a sip."Mmmm. Dry and flinty is my favorite combination in a white." She nodded toward the living room, "Have you read all the books out there?"

"Most of them. I love reading. That was actually the hardest part about moving to another country. I had to leave most of my books here."

"Are you glad to be back?"

"That's a complicated question. But first, you owe me the story of your life."

He arranged the food on plates. They sat in his cheerful kitchen pulling off hunks of focaccia and cheese and sipping the pale, golden wine.

"Where did you grow up? Any family other than this brother I've been hearing about?"

"I'm a genuine Yankee— grew up in Norwich, Vermont. Just my one straight-laced, disapproving brother. I was the kid with bright pink hair and thrift-shop clothes in high school who hung out with the artsy crowd. My father was an art history professor at Dartmouth, and my mother taught at the local elementary school. Then he got offered a position at Harvard around the time I started college, so they moved down here."

Luc made a frame with his hands.

"What are you doing?"

"Trying to picture you with pink hair."

"I looked great. I may dye it that color again. It sure would liven up Zoning board meetings."

Luc grinned as he broke off some tiny champagne grapes and added them to her plate. "Go on, Pinky."

She narrowed her eyes at him. "I stayed up at Dartmouth to major in Visual Studies. They had a good architecture program in theVis Stud department, and architecture had all the elements I liked about studio art, but it could actually affect people's lives. I was so idealistic then. I was going to design beautiful low-income housing." Iris smiled at the memory of her innocent idealism.

"I remember my first day at Harvard GSD. The other students seemed so sure of themselves and so worldly. Have you ever been inside the GSD building? It's almost all open inside, so you have several levels of drafting tables overlooking each other. The new students were fighting over desks. Somehow, I ended up with a desk next to Ellie's. We shared that look of 'What the hell have I gotten myself into?' and bonded right then."

"The December before I graduated, my parents' car crashed into a tree while driving back to Norwich to see friends." Her voice clouded. "They hit some black ice and were killed instantly."

Luc touched her hand.

She stopped speaking for a few minutes, then began again. "My brother, Stirling, had been living with them in the house on Washington Avenue, so he stayed on there."

"GSD was like boot camp, but I was glad to have something to throw myself into. World War III could have broken out and it wouldn't have registered inside the studio. After graduation, I was revved up to tackle the architect's Mecca—New York City. I loved being there. My job was high-powered. I had an exciting social life. But after a few years I wanted a place to put down roots. I wanted to live in a city—just not that large and impersonal a city. So I came back to Cambridge and reconnected with Ellie. Still, I felt withdrawal symptoms for a long time. Then a few years later, I met a guy and got married. It didn't last long. So… that's my life."

Luc considered her over his wine glass. "You sure slid over that last part quickly. I think I got whiplash."

She glanced down at her watch. "Oh, god, it's two! I have to meet my new client in Newton at two-thirty. I'll catch you later." Iris ran out of the kitchen, turned around, ran back, and kissed Luc a second time, this time quickly. Then she was gone.

***

Iris didn't know how to explain the embarrassment that had been her marriage. She'd been old enough— 30—to have known better than to marry Christopher after knowing him for only six months. She had been mesmerized by his perfect facade, his compatible background. It had seemed spontaneous, even romantic, to marry while the first blush was still on the romance. In retrospect, it was just naïve. Iris hated to have to think of herself as naïve.

Dashing Christopher had turned out to be a vacuous, coke-snorting narcissist. He had gotten fired from his investment banking job four months into the wedding. His new routine became collecting unemployment, reading the paper all morning at Starbucks, then drinking and pontificating with his buddies at the Forest Café until late in the evening. Sometimes he wouldn't come home until the next morning, Iris fuming at the breakfast table.

"You're not good enough in bed to be a gigolo!" she had shouted at him during one of their last fights. She had filed for divorce before their first anniversary.

CHAPTER 28

Ellie recognized Rachel in the lobby of the Inn at Harvard. They had met in the Registrar's office when she had helped Ellie get her transcript for her Ph.D. application. She looked more or less the same, her brown hair still waist-length with heavy bangs, but she now wore an expression of fatigue and worry. They crossed Mass Ave to the Café Pamplona for lunch.

"I can't believe this place is still here," Rachel said.

"Our local Brigadoon where Bow Street crosses Arrow Street," Ellie confirmed.

They approached the red clapboard house, dwarfed by neighboring apartment buildings. All the other funky restaurants from their graduate school days: Elsie's, the old Casablanca, the Blue Parrot, the Orson Welles and the Wursthaus, had been driven out by the high rents in Harvard Square.

"Let's eat inside. These outdoor tables aren't very inviting with diesel fumes from the passing buses," Actually, Ellie didn't want anyone to see her talking with Rachel after Iris's warning the day before.

Descending a few steps, they entered a semi-underground cave with bright yellow walls. The ceiling height couldn't have been an inch over seven feet.

"This headroom is definitely not to code," Ellie muttered as they sat down. A pony-tailed waitress drifted over to hand them menus, vacantly pointing out the specials on the board.

Rachel slumped in her chair. "I met with that tall, skinny cop this morning and he still doesn't know who killed Will. I just don't understand this, Ellie. Who would want to murder my husband? He was an architect, not a politician. He didn't have enemies. Are you sure Iris didn't do it?"

"I'm sure." Ellie said, smiling sympathetically. "But from what you said about a phone call, the killer must have been someone else going to the Friday dinner. And now Norman's been murdered as well. That couldn't be coincidence."

"The cop told me about that. I can't believe it. Are you sure it's not Iris? I heard she was out at his house when it happened."

"No, Iris just found him *after* it happened and she's the one who called the police." Ellie had to get Rachel off that track. "Did Will keep in touch with any of his old classmates?"

"Not really. Will didn't want anything to do with most of them, other than C.C. Those two were great buds. Will would stay with her whenever he was in New York on business. She can be hysterical, you know."

"Could C.C. and Will have had business dealings together—maybe going in together on one of Will's developments?"

"Will didn't have personal projects. He only did stuff through work and there's a guy in his office who does all the money arrangements. Besides, C.C. got a loft in New York and I think all her money went to that."

"How about Adam and Alyssa? Did he keep up with them? After all, Will and Adam were roommates for most of graduate school."

The waitress-waif materialized from nowhere. To her expectant look and poised pen Ellie said "I'll have the grape leaves and a grenadine soda. The sodas are made with real syrup here, Rachel."

"I'm not very hungry. Just a lemon soda for me." The waitress dematerialized.

Rachel's expression turned pensive. "Sure, we invited them to our wedding because they invited us to theirs, but the friendship seemed to fizzle out after graduation."

"Why? Did something happen?"

"I was just getting to know Will around then, but I think it had something to do with that guy who died at your graduation party. Will told me he saw Adam come back to the apartment later that night with the dead guy's backpack. I remember the story because it was a Star Trek backpack and I used to be a major Trekkie."

"Maybe Adam picked it up from the graduation party and didn't know what to do with it."

"No, it was later on that night. Will was packing up his stuff to move out. He saw Adam creep into his room with it, then shut the door. Will looked in again to make sure while Adam was in the shower."

"Why would Adam want Carey's backpack? It's not like any of us had money. I don't get it. Wait a minute. Does this have anything to do with that drugged brownie at the graduation party?"

"Oh yeah, that. Adam wanted to get Carey to eat a hash brownie. It was a joke to get back at Carey for getting all the good crits. They thought he would make a fool of himself because his system was really wired. But Adam got too stoned to do it, so he made Will do it. Then I guess the guy flipped out and there was that awful accident. But Will figured that Adam's taking the dead guy's back-pack was too much. It was like stealing from the dead, know what I mean? At least I think that's why things petered out with them. We got together a few times that summer, but after we moved out to the West Coast, we never saw them again. Which was fine by me—not to have to hang out with little-Miss-Chanel-sunglasses anymore."

"Rachel, did you tell Detective Malone about the backpack business? It might have something to do with Will's murder."

She thought for several minutes. "How could it? If Will never said anything to the cops in 20 years about Adam taking it, why would Adam worry about it now?

And actually kill Will? I can't see it. It would be Will's word against Adam's. Anyway, the skinny cop said that Adam and Alyssa had an alibi for Friday afternoon. They used a credit card at some gas station when they were driving up on Friday afternoon. So it wasn't them."

"Really? That's interesting. Did they ever find Will's cell phone?"

"No. It seems like whoever killed Will knew what he was doing—like some professional assassin. It's hard to think of one of my husband's Harvard classmates that way," Rachel said.

Ellie made a wry face. "Not if you knew them."

CHAPTER 29

"**H**e's definitely worth shaving my legs for," Iris concluded.

"Now don't forget my role in this. I had to use a cattle prod to get you to make a move."

Ellie's front door banged shut. Mack deposited his briefcase on the counter, kissed his wife, and held Iris at arm's length to examine her. "How's the patient? Got some fan mail I hear."

"Yuck, yuck. I'm fine. Luc smothered the flames before they could do much damage."

"And, Mack," Ellie called out. "Luc's passed Iris' taste test."

"I beg your pardon?"

"She saw his place today and it's a testament to chic understatement," Ellie said as she moved Mack's briefcase to the floor. "I know you'll find this hard to

Susan Cory

believe, dear, but some men actually have the taste gene and know how to pick up after themselves." She turned to rummage around in the freezer.

"I'm starting to wonder about this guy. He's gotta have some flaws." He looked at Iris expectantly, but she gave an exaggerated shrug.

"Sorry Mack, no discernible faults— at least so far. And, I have a gem of a new client. Life is good, other than the recent attempt on my life."

"Iris just stopped by to tell me about her romantic lunch with Luc. Then I was telling her about *my* lunch with Rachel. I learned from her that Adam stole Carey's backpack after he died—he must have broken into Carey's apartment and taken it. Will saw it on Adam's bed, not that Will ever bothered to tell this to the police back then. It was Adam's idea to drug Carey so he was probably the one who pushed him over the balcony."

"Whoa, slow down. Did you call Detective Malone? Did Rachel tell him about this? And do we think that means Adam also killed Will and Norman? He certainly sounds villainous enough. Maybe Will was finally going to tell someone about this."

"Like me, when he set up that meeting for Friday?" Iris said.

"Could be. Maybe Adam found out that he was about to be exposed at long last," Mack said.

"There are a couple of hitches with that theory." Iris said. "For one thing, it's not much of a threat. Will couldn't prove that the backpack had been Carey's. And even if he could have, it wouldn't necessarily follow that Adam had pushed Carey. Also, Adam's alibi for Friday afternoon was confirmed—some gas receipt from their car ride up at the critical time. So he couldn't have killed Will. At least, that's what Detective Malone told Rachel."

"I hate that… just when things are starting to make sense, the likely perp comes up with an alibi. This is a real stumper." Mack went to the refrigerator and pulled out a bottle of wine. "But this envelope bomb business changes everything. Please promise me that you'll both leave any sleuthing outside of these four walls to the police?"

Ellie and Iris both nodded. He placed three glasses on the counter and poured. Offering Ellie her glass, he asked, "So, how is Rachel holding up?"

"She's a mess and upset with the police that they haven't found Will's killer yet. She's taking his body to Rhode Island on Wednesday, as soon as the ME releases it."

"Oh, and speaking of the ME," Mack said, sitting at the table and sliding Iris her glass, "she let me know that the pre-lim on Norman suggests that he was killed with the same weapon as Will—a syringe of succinylcholine. Only, with Norman, it looks like there was also a struggle. There were bruises on his neck and arms. Will might have been taken by surprise."

"I've never heard of that drug. Where do you find it, Mack?" Ellie asked.

"Anesthesiologists use it, mainly for relaxing a patient's muscles when a tube needs to be inserted down a throat. It's not a common thing to use to kill someone. To have it used twice in one weekend—well, it's clearly the same guy."

"Do you know if they found the syringes?" Iris asked.

"They found the second needle. It had rolled under a table in Norman's kitchen and still had some of the drug left in it. That's how they figured out what had killed him. 'Sux' is hard to detect after it breaks down in a body, so they might not have figured it out otherwise."

"You're kidding. Norman was killed in his kitchen? I might have missed walking in on the killer by minutes," Iris moaned. "Did this all really just happen yesterday?"

"Thank god you didn't get there any sooner," her friend added.

"This reunion has turned into a bloodbath." Iris gnawed at her thumbnail. "Two murders, an envelope bomb and who knows how many verbal assaults."

CHAPTER 30

Tuesday morning, Iris received a phone call from Norman's assistant, Claire, while she was midway through the morning *Globe*.

"Hi Iris. How awful for you that you found Norman's body. How are you doing?"

"I'm trying to put it out of my mind, but thanks for asking. How are things over there? Has someone stepped in temporarily to run things?"

"Yes, the Vice-President, Mr. Dunn, will be in charge until the Board can find a new CEO. But Norman's attorney called and said that his estate will be selling Norman's new house out in Lincoln."

Iris groaned.

"I know. After all that work, it's a real shame. The Attorney said it's important that all the work done is verified and the workers paid so that no one can put a lien on the property. There are a ton of receipts here on Norman's desk and I was wondering if you could help me sort through them."

"Sure. How soon do you want to tackle it?"

"How soon can you get here?"

An hour later Iris and Claire were in Norman's office dividing his papers into neat piles on the floor and desk.

"I should go through these invoices to make sure we don't double pay anyone," Iris said. "And I don't want any invoices to get lost in the shuffle. What's this manila envelope?"

"Oh, I think those are receipts from the tile installer. If you could just confirm them first, I'll pay him. By the way," continued a newly chatty Claire, "the funeral is going to be held on Saturday at 10 at Mount Auburn Cemetery. All of us from Norman Meeker Enterprises are getting paid overtime to go."

"Boy, that was pulled together fast. Will they be done with the autopsy by then? Who did the organizing anyway?"

"The Medical Examiner's office promised that we could have the body by Saturday. Norman had organized all the details for the funeral with his lawyer—right down to the type of casket, flowers, and songs he wanted. Do you believe it? By the way, don't bother sending any flowers. He only wants white Calla lilies."

"Wait a minute. Are you telling me that Norman knew he was going to die?"

"I'm sure he didn't expect to die so soon, but preparation was his motto. You must have noticed that when you worked with him. He viewed life as one big chess game, and he was always strategizing three moves ahead. He left complete instructions for his funeral, including who he wanted there."

"That's bizarre. He can't make people show up... can he?"

"No, but overtime will draw an enthusiastic response from the employees here. I don't know why the rest of the people on the list would come."

"Oh, Claire—I almost forgot. Do you have a phone number for Norman's ex, Barb?"

"Sure. Can you wait a sec?" Claire went to her desk in the outer office.

Iris finished shoving receipts into her tote bag and followed after her. She idly picked up a postcard propped against a picture frame on Claire's desk. "This is the De Young Museum by Herzog and de Meuron in San Francisco. Have you seen it in the flesh?"

Claire looked over at the image." Oh, that's a postcard Norman had thrown out. I kept it because I thought the building looked cool. Someday I want to get out there to see it."

Iris flipped over the card. "Looking forward to our talk on Friday—Renno."

It was from Will. He had been excited about coming to the reunion and chatting with Norman at the dinner. Sadness settled over her.

"I'm not sure that this number is still current, but this is what's in the file for Barb."

As Iris left, Claire called out to her, "See you at the funeral. You're on the list."

Not if I can help it, Iris thought.

CHAPTER 31

Iris spent early Tuesday afternoon out at her new Chestnut Hill job taking measurements for the "as built" drawings of a penthouse. Her client, Lillian Butterworth, was a widow ready to make big changes in her life. She had sold the family Victorian, replacing it with a modern penthouse whose wrap-around windows gave her a view of the Boston skyline. She wanted Iris to tear out walls and reconfigure the space to be more of a loft. Iris loved adventurous clients. This would be a fun job.

Back at her Cambridge office, Iris ripped off a piece of yellow tracing paper and taped it to her drafting board. Then, adding up the overall measurements of the penthouse, she marked them on the paper, using a quarter-inch, triangular scale. As she started to sketch in the outer walls of the space, the phone rang.

"Hi, Iris. This is Barb. I got your message. It's been awhile."

"Oh, hi, Barb. I'm sorry about Norman." Iris had forgotten Barb's nasal upstate New York accent. "How have you been? I didn't see you at the reunion. I wondered if we could talk."

"I didn't feel like rehashing graduate school, so I avoided the reunion, but I could meet with you. When and where is good? The kids are away at boarding school, so my schedule's pretty open."

"Do you know where the Paradise Café is in Cambridge, near Porter Square?"

"I've heard of it. I'm sure I can GPS it. It's on Mass Ave, right?"

"Right. Does 4 o'clock work for you? We could get coffee. Sorry again about Norman."

"Don't be. I'm not. See you at 4."

**

By the time Iris arrived at the café Barb was already seated with a coffee cup at her mouth. The years had not been kind to her. In a tunic with loose pants, she looked dowdier than her years.

"It sure is impossible to park around here, Iris."

"Sorry about that. I usually walk here. So, how are you?" A hug did not look expected or welcome. She racked her brain for some bridge-twenty-years small talk and came up with "I hadn't realized that you and Norman had kids. How old are they?"

"Thirteen and fifteen—both boys. It's a horrendous age, early teens." She proceeded to detail their latest obnoxious scenes. As it became clear that Barb was just warming up to her topic, Iris held up a time-out finger and ran to the counter to get a decaf.

"Have you got any booze to slip in there?" she asked Louise.

Louise glanced over at Barb and raised a brow. "Nothing that would mix with coffee. Want me to interupt you with an emergency or something?"

"No, but thanks for the thought."

As Iris returned to the table, Barb started right in again with "Norman never mentions his sons. They make him feel old. I guess I should use the past tense for him now."

"I'm sure his death has been hard for them."

"Not really. I haven't told them yet. Their shrinks can help them cope when they get back from school. He was never what you would call an involved parent."

Time to pry Barb off of this subject.

"So, have you been working in architecture since school? You've probably had your hands full with two kids."

"I had my hands full with Norman. He was such a control freak. Everything had to be done his particular way. In the beginning it was kind of exciting, being with someone so smart and ambitious. But once he got fixated on these inventions of his, he became obsessed. They were all about saving energy. He was ahead of his time—I'll give him that."

"Where did Norman pick up this interest? I don't remember him having an engineering or science background."

"No, but he recognized a business need when he saw it. You probably remember, when we entered architecture school in '85, the energy crisis was still a big deal. While we were in school, that crisis may have died down, but the handwriting was on the wall. Norman saw the need for products that depended less on oil, or used oil more efficiently. OPEC could just raise prices, or embargo oil at any time, and we'd be screwed again."

"But how did he have the technical knowledge to invent all those products?"

"He did what all businessmen do—he bought the know-how. His first partner was a guy named Jim Bennett. He was the one with the engineering smarts. Norman's ego broke up the partnership, of course, but only after he had gotten what he needed from Jim."

"Can you think of anyone, this Jim Bennett or anyone else, who might have hated him enough to want to kill him?"

"Well, Norman was ruthless in business, but that isn't usually enough to get you killed or Wall Street would be littered with bodies. There were times when *I* could have killed him, but I didn't—probably a lack of imagination on my part. We've been divorced for a year now, so I've had time to chill out. How come you're so interested in finding out who killed him? I'm sure the police are working on it. They called to ask me a bunch of questions."

"I'm just curious. I was working on his house for almost a year. I was just wondering about Meeker Enterprises and who would take over now."

"Well, he always surrounded himself with yes-men. He couldn't delegate to save his life. He was afraid of a power play. I seriously doubt he left a strong candidate to succeed him."

Iris tried to think of a useful question. Something Barb had said had sounded relevant. Oh, yes. "Do you by any chance know Jim Bennett's phone number?"

"I can probably find it in an old address book at home. I'll e-mail it to you." They exchanged a few architecture school memories before Barb rose.

"I've gotta run now, Iris. Take care."

"You too." Iris wandered back to the counter where Louise sat reading a book while she waited for customers.

"Hey, Louise, is Luc in the kitchen now?"

"Um, he should be back soon, Iris. I think he's picking up Allegra from her exercise class."

CHAPTER 32

Iris and Ellie sat side by side in the pedicure chairs at the Beauty Connection on Mass Ave. Ellie, eyes closed, had her chair on the massage setting and kept arching her back as the rollers undulated.

"See, Ellie. I told you that this would happen. He's already running around with some hussy/chef named Allegra. She's probably 25. Who names their child 'Allegra' anyway? Is that the new Tiffany? You know, that looks a bit obscene—what you're doing."

Ellie rolled up the *People Magazine* on her lap and gave Iris a swat.

"No move, miss!" and "Stay still!" rang out from their glaring pedicurists.

"Sorry," "Sorry," they responded.

"Where have you been, Iris? Tiffany went out with shoulder pads and white pantyhose."

"White pantyhose are out?"

Ellie managed to give her a look with one eye closed.

"Now we can never hang out in the Paradise again," Iris said. "You've ruined our morning ritual! And they have the best cappuccinos in Cambridge!"

"Oh, chill out. Allegra is probably middle-aged, overweight and doesn't own a car. Luc, being the gentleman that he is, is probably giving her a ride. You're acting more like a drama queen than Raven. Speaking of whom, have you made her Lady Baltimore cake? She says she's not coming home unless we can have it at dinner tomorrow night."

"Fine, fine. That's all I'm good for anyway—my baking skills."

Ellie said "That's right. Go home after this and make that cake!"

***

Iris could hear the phone ringing as she opened the kitchen door. She got to it before the answering machine kicked in.

"Hi, Cara, it's Luc. Louise said I missed you."

Blessed words: he missed her. "Hi. I was at the café with Norman's ex-wife. She was filling me in on her life with him. He sure sounds like a pain to live with."

"I thought you were going to lie low after Sunday's ambush."

"I wanted to tie up this loose end. I figure I'm okay if I stay away from the prime suspects. What have you been up to today? What's that noise in the background?"

"That's the pasta machine. I'm prepping for Allegra tonight but don't need to stay late. Why don't you stop by at nine? We could stroll down to Chez Henri for a late bite. Their chef Paul and I are friendly competitors."

"I'd love to, but I'll be busy tonight making a Lady Baltimore cake for Raven's homecoming tomorrow. It can take forever to get the damned boiled white icing done right, depending on how many times I miss the precise 'soft-ball' moment and have to start over."

"Yeah, that drives me nuts too."

"Very funny. Maybe you'll get to try some if you're good. Are you cooking tomorrow night? Want to come to this dinner at Ellie's?"

"I'd love to but I'm on duty through Friday night. We're working on new menu ideas. How about dinner Saturday night?"

"You're on. And if you're lucky, I might just save you a piece of cake."

"Great. And I'm going to pay particular attention to the icing. No pressure though."

CHAPTER 33

Raven's black hair and huge brown eyes echoed her mother's coloring. But she was tall where her mother was short. As a baby, her long thin neck, tiny round mouth and thatch of fluffy hair made her resemble a baby bird peeking out of its nest.

Now, as Iris entered Ellie's kitchen and saw mother and daughter preparing dinner, Raven looked more like a rare, exotic bird. Dressed in brightly colored layers of thrift-shop finds—henley, gypsy blouse, long, flowered dress, shrug, and black motorcycle boots—she had the natural chic of a runway model decked out in couture.

"You made the cake!" Raven enthused as Iris set it quickly on the counter so it wouldn't get crushed in their hug.

"Of course I did. It's our version of the fatted calf for the prodigal daughter. So, how's the college kid? Any new tats or piercings?"

"Nope. I'm being rebellious. I even took out my nose ring. It's too cliché."

"Just don't rebel too much and become a skinhead."

"Like that would happen. I wouldn't be allowed back to the People's Republik of Cambridge."

"Damn straight. When did you get home?"

"This afternoon. Mom picked me up with my stuff. We had to tie some of the bigger canvases to the roof of the car."

"I can't wait to see what you're painting these days."

"Mom says you're dating some hunky young stud and getting letter bombs. That's so cool!"

"A hunky young stud? Who's talking about me?" Mack sailed in cradling a big paper bag. He went over to hug Raven. "Ah, bliss. I have all my women together again," he said, stretching his arms wide to include Iris. Then he kissed Ellie and said "University Wines had a nice, not-too-sweet Riesling on special, so I got a few bottles to try. Will that do with your trout, my sweet?"

Okay, so maybe not all relationships sucked, Iris thought.

Over dinner, they dissected the murders.

Raven posed some questions: "What if Adam flew up to Boston early on Friday and Alyssa drove the car up? Did the police actually say that it was his signature on the gas receipt? Or maybe she forged his signature? And have they found Norman's cell phone? Had the murderer set up a meeting with Norman, or did the murderer follow him to the house?"

They were all caught up in private eye mode. Raven continued, "We need to ask these suspects more questions. We should be able to figure this out. As Sherlock Holmes always said, 'When you have eliminated the impossible, whatever remains, however improbable, must be the truth'."

Mack held up his hands, palms out. "It's fine for us to speculate around the dining table about this thing. But Iris's letter bomb yesterday was no joke. She could have been badly burned. There's some maniac out there, and he or she has killed two, possibly three, people already. So, all of you, please promise me that you are not going to do any more snooping. The police are going to find this person. There must be fingerprints or DNA somewhere around Norman's house, even if Will's site was clean. It takes at least 48 hours to get DNA results back from the lab, so they should be closing in on the killer soon."

Ellie, Raven and Iris eyed each other around the table. Three minds mulled over how they could find clues while staying off a murderer's radar.

"We'll keep our heads down, Pop. And don't worry, my next karate test is for my brown belt."

"Oh, you kept up with that?" Iris had taken Raven along during her high-school years to the dojo where she herself had practiced.

"I found a good sensei in Providence this spring and started up again. We should practice sparring, Aunt Iris."

"I haven't sparred since you went off to college. I wonder how much I remember." Iris had immersed herself in Karate after her divorce as a psychological exercise to make herself feel stronger. After hitting 40 and earning her brown belt, she tapered off her training rather than staying on track for her black belt.

"Time for the cake," Mack announced as he got up to clear plates.

"I've had cravings for this all through exam week."

A Lady Baltimore cake is more than the sum of its parts. The alchemy of home-made white cake with boiled white icing into which pecans, dried figs and raisins have been mixed is anything but bland. The icing hardens, balancing the chewiness of the raisins and figs with the nuts. Conversation went on hold for the next five minutes. And three of the four minds thought about murder.

CHAPTER 34

The next morning, Wednesday, Iris floated between consciousness and sleep as she heard the familiar drone: "Street cleaning! No parking on the even side of the street. Your car will be tagged and towed." The message looped continuously from the speaker of the Public Works truck as it navigated through the neighborhood, warning residents April through November of this Cambridge monthly ritual. Iris dragged herself to the window. Her Jeep was nestled in its spot in the driveway, as she knew it would be, but the warning always compelled her to check.

This city is such a quirky place, she thought as she stumbled downstairs to the kitchen to make coffee. Did other cities have street cleaning announcements?

Coming back here from New York had not been an easy decision. Choosing to live in her parent's house had been an even tougher one. Their absence from the grand Victorian had felt like a dull ache. But, bit by bit, she had made the house her own. Starting in the garden with its unforgiving clay soil, she had coaxed hardy rose bushes and shade-tolerant hostas to bloom. The Goodwill truck had carted away the fussy living room furniture, leaving emptiness behind as Iris saved up for two black leather Corbusier chairs and a simple, sleek sofa to take their place. She started taking on small architecture projects—master bath and kitchen renovations, working from the sunniest room on the first floor in the turret. Puttering around on her own house continued until, one day, she realized that her parents no longer inhabited the shadows.

By mid-morning Iris was in her office sketching design ideas on yellow tracing paper superimposed over her "as built" drawings. Her first schematic design meeting with Lillian Butterworth was scheduled for the next day. She liked to present several possible solutions and discuss their merits before zeroing in on one to develop. If she had time, she'd freehand some perspective sketches to help Lillian visualize the options.

Bent over her drafting table, she started at the sound of the phone. "Reid Associates."

"Oh, Iris, it's C.C.. Do you have a minute?"

"Sure, what's up?" she tried to sound calm, remembering that C.C. was a possible suspect for Norman's murder.

"I just read Norman's obituary in the *Times* yesterday. God, I'm so freaked. What is it about this GSD class? Are we cursed?"

"It *is* pretty incredible."

"Have you heard anything from the police? Do they have an idea who's been doing this?"

"Not that I know about."

"I'm calling because I'd like your advice. There's something I remembered and I don't know if it could be important. It's something Will said to me last month. I thought I'd run this by you since you seem to be playing Nancy Drew."

Why was everything C.C. said to her mildly insulting? "Okay. What was it?"

"He asked if I thought Norman might want to be an investor in a school he wanted to turn into condos in San Francisco. He wanted to ask him about it at the reunion."

"That sounds pretty innocent to me. Norman could always say no."

"Well, he went on to say he had thought of some way to convince Norman to back him."

"What do you mean 'some way to convince him?'" Iris was trying to control her impatience.

"That's just it. I wasn't really paying much attention."

"Well how did he say it? Did he sound devious or earnest?"

"Um, self-satisfied."

"What leverage could he possibly have had on Norman?"

"That's the exact word he used—leverage."

"But Will never made it to the reunion, so how could he have discussed anything with Norman? And now they're both dead, so the killer must be a third person"

Iris saw Sheba lumbering over with a ball. She avoided eye contact. "Could someone have wanted to prevent Norman from investing with Will?"

"They were both killed, so do you mean someone who wanted to buy the school himself?" C.C. asked. "Maybe it looked like a lucrative deal and someone was trying to eliminate the competition."

"By murdering them—even someone who was merely a potential investor? That sounds far-fetched," Iris said.

"I don't think Will was that savvy about making money. I doubt that he could have stumbled on some project that would inspire that level of greed."

"Still, this is a connection between two murder victims that the police won't know about unless Rachel's mentioned it. And she may not even know about it. You need to call Detective Malone. He'll need you to give a signed statement about it. I can give you his number. He's the one who's putting the pieces together." She retrieved his card from under the answering machine and read off the information.

"Can't you tell him, Iris? You're already involved."

"It would be hearsay coming from me. Will spoke to you. Besides, I'm staying out of this now. Are you coming up on Saturday for Norman's funeral? You can make an appointment to talk with Malone then. Two birds, one stone."

"Funny. I hadn't been planning on flying back up there. I'll think about it. Bye."

Iris cracked her knuckles as she mulled over the phone call. What leverage could Will have thought he had on Norman?

CHAPTER 35

A few hours later Iris finished her final sketch. She decided to go through the pile of receipts that Claire had asked her to verify. She had worked her way to the middle of the pile when she came upon a manila envelope that said *Linc* on the front. Claire had thought that these were receipts from the tile subcontractor, Iris remembered. She unwound the twist string and out fell a cassette. Huh? Why would a sub be submitting this? Seeing nothing else inside, she looked for a label on the tape. No label. What the hell was this and why was it on a cassette? She didn't even own a cassette player anymore. They'd all either broken or been tossed out with the advent of CDs. Damn. Should she just return it to Claire and let her figure out its relevance to the Lincoln renovation? Now she was starting to get curious.

A rapping sound coming from the direction of the kitchen interrupted her thoughts. Through her office's framed opening she could see Ellie and Raven at the kitchen door.

"We just finished a yoga class and want to drag you to the Paradise for a coffee break. It's gorgeous out! Oh, here's my favorite doggy. How're you doin', little girl?" Raven squatted on the floor and rubbed Sheba under the chin. The dog was on her back in a second.

Twenty minutes later, in the Paradise, Iris and Ellie ate *sfogliatelle* with their iced decaf lattes. The shell-shaped Italian pastry was a house specialty. Raven stuck to chai and a muffin. She asked Iris, "Did you ever have the yoga teacher who tells you to imagine a marble getting sucked into your belly button? What was her name, Mom—Summer? Autumn?"

"The marble's supposed to go through the belly-button, I think. Why does that image bother you so much?" Ellie asked. "She's just trying to give us visual types a way to use the correct muscles."

"It doesn't make any sense as an image," Iris said. "Why doesn't she just say 'suck in your gut'? But forget Spring, or whatever her name is. I want to tell you about the phone call I just had from C.C."

"Is she going to put Norman's house in the magazine?"

"Yeah, I think so, but that's not why she called." Iris told them the leverage story.

"That is so weird—Will thought that he had something to hold over Norman's head? It's got to have been something from 20 years ago. Why would he wait until now to use it?"

"Maybe there was nothing he wanted from Norman before this and all the reunion hoopla jogged his memory."

"Hmm. This might be important. But do we believe C.C.? She might be making this up. Neither Will or Norman is around to object."

"I'm wondering how can we find out about her whereabouts on Sunday. I tried to talk her into coming up for the funeral so she could tell the leverage story to Detective Malone. Maybe I should go to this funeral myself. I did just finish designing Norman's house and I did find his body."

"Uh-huh. Why do I think it's curiosity rather than loyalty driving this sudden change of heart?" Ellie glanced over at the coffee counter. "Do I want another pastry? Better not. Maybe Will told her what this leverage was, so she killed Will and tried to blackmail Norman with it herself. When he wouldn't give in, she killed him."

"Oooh—I like that. It's very tidy." Iris said. "I could see her killing Norman, but I don't know about Will. I think they really were friends. By the way, do you have a cassette player? I found a tape among the Lincoln receipts that I should probably check out."

Raven was listening avidly, trying to get up to speed on the cast of characters. "I have an old boom box somewhere in my room. I could dig it up for you." She looked around and asked loudly "Where's Luc? I want to meet the hunky chef."

Louise, overhearing, grinned. "He's in the kitchen," she called over to them. "You can go on back. I'm sure he won't mind."

Iris had never seen the Paradise's kitchen and wasn't sure that she wanted to walk in on Allegra and Luc unannounced. But Raven had scrambled to her feet and dragged her mother by the arm so Iris followed.

The kitchen looked like it belonged on a submarine. It was small, gleaming with stainless steel, and highly organized. Tom Waits growled incongruously over the sound system. A woman stood with her back to them, stirring something on the stove. Luc was cleaning some type of bivalve at another work counter. He looked up and beamed. "Ladies, welcome!"

Before he could continue, Iris blurted out, "Louise sent us back so Raven could meet you."

Luc rubbed his hands together under the faucet, wiped them on his apron, then offered one to Raven. "Nice to meet you." He gestured to the woman beside him. "And I'd like to introduce all of you to my new chef, Allegra."

The woman looking up to greet them resembled a cherubic Italian grandmother.

Iris and Ellie exchanged quick glances then both smiled warmly.

CHAPTER 36

By Thursday afternoon, with Barb's help, Iris had tracked Jim Bennett to an eco-tech firm in Cambrige's Kendall Square neighborhood. Proximity to M.I.T. had spawned a veritable village of research-and-development companies. The lobby receptionist had her name on his list, so Iris was directed to a bank of elevators. She was disgorged directly into a large open-plan office filled with walled-off cubicles. There was no internal receptionist, so Iris popped her head over the closest partition.

"Do you know where I could find Jim Bennett please?"

The man stood up and yelled out "Jim! There's a lady here." Then he resumed frowning at his computer monitor, ignoring her.

A tall, pale man with large aviator glasses scurried in through a door at the rear of the room.

"Sorry. Sorry. I was back in the lab."

"I appreciate you meeting with me, Mr. Bennett," Iris said, as he led her to a small conference room.

"I'm not sure there's much I can tell you about Norman Meeker. I read about his death in the papers. You said that you went to architecture school with him and designed him a house. Were you friends, then?"

"Well, no, I wouldn't put it like that. I was just asking Barb how Norman had become interested in this field. It seems to draw people with either a more technical or a more altruistic background than Norman had."

Jim snorted.

"No pussyfooting around the truth! I like that. You're absolutely right, Ms. Reid. Norman's main interest in all these brilliant inventions was their bottom line. I had the chemistry and engineering background to develop some of them. Others were way too far out there to be practical. Mind you, this was in the early nineties. The twenty-first century may have caught up to some of the ideas by now."

"But I don't understand where the initial concepts came from. You speak as though you didn't generate them yourself."

"Ah, I see your confusion. 'The mystery of the blue notebook' is how I used to think of it. Norman had gotten his hands on a notebook that was filled with brilliant scribblings. At first, he tried to pass it off as his own work. He'd even hang out in the lab talking with the technicians about various experiments. But it was clear the guy didn't know a thing about science, much less the kind of visionary theoretical stuff that was in this notebook. I wish I could meet whoever actually wrote it. Hell, I'd hire him in a minute. The ideas all focused on ways to harness nature to solve environmental problems that hadn't even reached most people's consciousness as issues. For example, he was postulating ways to convert various waste products into energy sources or fertilizer. The idea of using the earth's core temperature to heat and cool—that was from the notebook. Whoever wrote it was a genius."

"You said that you first saw this notebook in the early nineties?"

"That's right. Norman had just graduated from the B school and asked me to team up with him. That notebook launched Norman into the eco-entrepreneurial big time. He kept it under heavy wraps in his office safe when he wasn't allowing me little peeks at it, a few copied pages at a time. My job was to work out the manufacturing details to make the ideas feasible. We had no trouble getting venture and angel funding for projects like this. Those guys lapped it up. But I eventually got my fill of working with Norman. His paranoia and need for control got to be too much for me, so I went out and started my own firm. It was a valuable experience, though. It jump-started my own thinking about these issues."

"The worth of this notebook—what kind of money are we talking about?"

"The inventions that came out of those ideas must have brought Norman profits in the billions. This field is enormously lucrative as oil becomes more of a political weapon in the Middle East."

Iris sat thinking for a minute. Profits in the billions. That's worth killing for. She needed to put this all together. Rising to leave she said, "Well, thanks for your time, Mr. Bennett."

"Um, maybe I could just ask *you* a question?" His ears were turning bright red. "Do you have Barb's phone number? I'd love to call with my condolences."

Iris read it off to him without mentioning that Barb was far from distraught. As she left she brooded on the fact that there would never be any more ideas coming from the author of that notebook.

CHAPTER 37

"Sheba! Walkies!" It was amazing how that word energized the dog, getting her to leap up mid-snore out of her den inside the fireplace. Iris relied on this daily stroll under the ancient trees, gazing out over the calm reservoir, to get her thoughts in order. Something had been tugging at the corner of her consciousness for most of this Friday morning.

Earlier, she had presented three schemes to Lillian Butterworth, showing sketches of each one and discussing pros and cons. But even as she helped her client choose which design to develop, she could feel a part of her brain racing on auto-search.

Raven's Sherlock Holmes quote floated into her mind. If you eliminated everything that was impossible, then whatever remained, however improbable, had to be the answer. Adam had stolen Carey's backpack. It must have contained Carey's notebook, the place he scribbled down his brilliant ideas, ideas like the ones that made Norman's fortune. Norman kept a notebook with brilliant inventions in his safe and mined their ideas for new products to manufacture under his firm's name. So Adam probably sold the notebook to Norman. That much made sense. But in the present day, she could imagine a motive for Norman to kill Adam, to try to hide his connection to the stolen notes of an inventor who had died under suspicious circumstances. This theory would jibe with Norman's recent campaign for respectability and prestige. Or maybe Adam was blackmailing Norman for more money. He probably compared how much Norman had paid him many years ago for the notebook to the billions that Norman had managed to make off it since then.

Ellie, Mack and Raven had been out at a movie the previous evening, but Iris had stayed up half the night putting this much together before coming to a stumbling block: These were both reasons for Norman to kill Adam, not the reverse. Norman was the golden goose and it was unlikely that he would expose Adam for theft, because he would implicate himself as well.

Did C.C. fit somewhere into this puzzle? Was she its mastermind? And if Adam was involved, did that mean that Alyssa was too? If there were four of these prima donnas working together, how did they ever keep this plot hushed up for all these years?

What about Will's murder? Maybe that was tied to his being Adam's roommate. If Rachel was to be believed, Will was not involved in the theft of the blue notebook—but he might have connected the dots.

Maybe someone assumed that he had been involved. Yet both murders used the same weapon, a hypodermic needle containing an uncommon drug. Since the murders happened two days apart, the chance of a copycat killer finding out exactly what the weapon was and reproducing it that quickly seemed unlikely.

Carey must have been murdered so his notebooks could be stolen. But why not just hire him for his ideas instead of killing him? He probably wouldn't have agreed to work for anyone else. Or maybe the theft was opportunistic after Carey actually did become disoriented while drugged and fall off the balcony.

Sheba had stopped walking and was rolling on the grass, massaging her back. The dog liked to punctuate her walk this way. Iris sat on a nearby bench, brain cells churning. Adam seemed to be the key to these murders. How could she get more information about his movements? She wanted to know more about his alibi for Friday. Maybe she could trade information with Detective Malone. But what did she know that he didn't?

She leaned back against the rough wood bench and let the weak June sun warm her face. An idea formed.

CHAPTER 38

"Hi, Arturo? It's Iris Reid. I got your phone number from the Reunion book, but I didn't see you there." From her office chair, Iris preemptively tossed a toy pig into the living room for Sheba.

"Oh, hey Iris. Yeah, I meant to go, but at the last moment, I had to bail. I came down with the flu last Friday. I'm only starting to feel human again today. What did I miss?"

"Just doddering, middle-aged versions of the same crazies from two decades ago. Oh, and a couple of murders. Will and Norman."

"Oof, I read about that in the papers. God. Have they found out who did it?"

"Not yet. Do you believe it— two of our classmates?"

"What do you think—it had something to do with the reunion? The papers didn't say much. I'm not feeling too compos mentis with all this flu med I'm on. Tell me, what's really going on?"

"I don't know, Arturo. I was there Friday night. Will never showed up. Then Norman was killed on Sunday. I actually found the body because I was supposed to help him with some punch list things for his new house."

"Yeah, yeah, I read that. You were his architect. Nightmare city for you."

"I can't figure out any connection between the two of them, can you?"

"No, they weren't really friends. I don't remember Norman having any friends other than Barb. Oh, those two got married, didn't they? She must be torn up about it."

"Not really. They were divorced. Did you talk with anyone from the reunion? I remember that you and Adam used to play squash a lot on the Dunster House courts."

"Oh, yeah. Those were the days. He had a key to Dunster House and we used to sneak onto their squash courts late at night."

"I remember hearing about those games. So you guys didn't stay in touch?"

"Wait. Wait. He called last weekend to try to set up a match with me for Sunday, but I was dead to the world by then."

"When did he call?"

"I think it was... Saturday. That's right, Saturday afternoon."

"Did he say anything about Will being killed?"

"Now that you mention it, he didn't—just asked if I was up for squash. Why are you asking all these questions about Adam? He's not involved in this, is he?"

"I have no idea. I was just looking for him on Sunday and Alyssa told me that he was playing squash with you. When you said you'd been sick, I wondered why she had told me that. Maybe he needed a break from her. Who knows? Anyway, I'm glad you're feeling better." Iris nestled the phone in her shoulder. Now she had her chip to trade. "Give me a call if you get up to Cambridge. Oh, and Arturo? If you talk to Adam again please don't mention that I was asking about the squash, okay?"

"No problem. Now I've got a question for you. I had this message on my desk when I got back to work today. A Cambridge cop named Malone left it. Do you know what that's about? I haven't called him yet."

"He's just calling about that squash game. I'll tell him. I need to talk to him anyway."

So Adam hadn't been playing squash when Norman was murdered. And he had lied about it—or Alyssa had lied for him. This information felt hot. It felt too dangerous to keep to herself. Someone had already tried to silence her. She flicked the button for a dial tone, then punched in the now-familiar number.

The detective told her to meet him at police headquarters in an hour.

***

When a uniformed cop escorted her up to his office on the third floor, Malone was talking on the phone, but motioned for her to sit down. Iris had never seen such an impersonal office—no family photos, no pictures on the wall, no knick-knacks, not even a coffee mug with his first name revealed—he might as well be in the Witness Protection Program. His desk was the desk of a workaholic—covered with files piled around a computer. She wondered if there was a file on her.

His voice was flat, professional. "So they're all gonna be there? Good. I want Corso to take the detail. Yeah, I'll be there too. Okay, good." He hung up and swiveled in his chair to face her.

"Ms. Reid, hello again. You've got some information for me?"

"Yes, I think I may have figured out how Adam Lincoln is a link between Will Reynolds and Norman Meeker."

"Go on," He sounded unimpressed.

She told him everything she knew or suspected. She also laid out the loose ends. Then she asked, "Since Adam's alibi for Sunday was bogus, isn't it possible the one for Friday was also faked—with or without his wife's help?"

Detective Malone pressed his palms together prayer-like at his mouth, the personification of close-mouthed. After a few long minutes, he came out of his reverie. "No, he got cash from an ATM at around three at a Mobil station in Connecticut, and both of them were on the security video."

"So even though Adam lied about his whereabouts on Sunday, even though he may have sold Norman a murdered classmate's notebook of inventions, you can't link him to Norman's murder?"

"It's like this, Ms. Reid. There's this pesky little detail that the District Attorney tells us we need to pay attention to called proof. Besides, Mr. Lincoln's alibi for Friday is solid and it's highly unlikely that we have two separate murderers running around using the identical method. Still, you've given us some information that may be useful. I'm glad you came to me instead of trying to confront Mr. Lincoln directly."

"I haven't been trying to confront these people! It's not my fault that Norman called me to his house or that I got a letter bomb. People call me and give me information because I'm someone they know. I'm passing this information along to you. I'm desperate for you to arrest the murderer before he succeeds in killing me... or Ellie."

"Calm down Ms. Reid. I appreciate that you have access to information people withhold from us and that you're reporting it to us. But if there's some way of getting people to talk to us directly, it would be safer for you."

"I've told C.C. to speak to you directly about the 'leverage' discussion with Will."

"Good. While we're discussing keeping a low profile, were you intending to go to Mr. Meeker's funeral tomorrow?"

"I haven't decided yet. Would it be dangerous to go?"

"I'm gonna be there with back-up, so it should be safe enough. I learned from Mr. Meeker's assistant that…" he squinted at his computer, "C.C., Adam, Alyssa, and Professor Broussard plan to be there too."

"I'm thinking I probably should go and pay my respects. I did just finish designing a house for him."

"Is that why his lawyer says he left you the Porsche?"

CHAPTER 39

Louise was humming as she set the tables for the
Friday night dinner crowd, working her way
around the one where her boss sat huddled in
deep discussion.

"So Adam was really stealing Carey's notebook, not
the backpack, so he could sell it to Norman." Iris
explained.

Ellie pried open a pistachio and asked, "But did
Adam just happen to be there when Carey fell and then
decide to take advantage of the accident, or was it
murder from the start?"

Luc continued, "How could Adam have known that
Norman would be willing to pay him a lot of money for
the notebook? Or were they in it together? Maybe
Norman put him up to stealing it."

"I called Carey's friend Patty this afternoon." Iris said. "At the reunion picnic, I had asked her if she knew of any connection between Carey and Will. This time I asked about a link between Carey and Norman. She remembered overhearing Norman offer Carey a job toward the end of our last semester. Carey turned him down, but Adam might have overheard this exchange and figured that Norman would be willing to pay for Carey's ideas if he couldn't hire the inventor himself."

"Still, Adam wouldn't necessarily have had to kill Carey to get the notebook," Luc pointed out as he refilled their glasses from a bottle of Meursault. "He could have just stolen it."

"But then Carey might have recognized some of his inventions after Norman started manufacturing them," Iris said. "Also, I'll bet that that weasel, Adam, just wanted to see Carey making a fool of himself for a change instead of making others feel like fools at their crits. Maybe Adam thought that he'd have time to retrieve the notebook while Carey came down off his high. Then again, maybe he couldn't resist giving him a shove when the two of them were alone on the balcony, in retaliation for Carey so easily designing circles around him," Iris conjectured.

"Okay, I see a link between Carey, Adam and Norman," Ellie said, "but how did Will fit into the picture? Why was he killed?"

"He was in Carey's studio so he might have overheard Norman's job offer too. He also saw Carey's backpack in Adam's room. Maybe he figured out the connection and let something drop about what he knew. Wait a minute. That must be the leverage he thought he had over Norman. He was planning on threatening to expose the source of Norman's business success unless Norman backed his condo deal."

"But Adam would be the only one who would be threatened enough by exposure to go on to murder Will. And that would only be true if Adam had pushed Carey and there was evidence to prove it. But Adam supposedly has a cast-iron alibi for the time of Will's murder," Ellie groaned. "This thing is a conundrum. It just keeps going round and round."

"We've got to be getting close to something. We've linked all four of them. We only need to break through Adam's damn alibi. By the way, Detective Malone said that Adam and Alyssa will be at the funeral tomorrow."

"Have you told Luc about that other thing—what Detective Malone said?"

"Uh, evidently Norman left me the Porsche in his will."

"You're kidding—why?" Luc raised his eyebrows. "I mean, I know he loved your design for his house. Was it gratitude, do you think?"

"It might be a kind of joke. I had told him I'd take it instead of my architectural fee. His attorney told the police it was a recent bequest. But Norman wasn't intending to die anytime soon. I imagine he thought he'd live another 40 years. I can't figure out what went on in his head. The car's a real beauty. It's a 1995 black 928, s-model, the hot one."

"I hope you'll give me a ride in it." Luc leaned slowly across the table. "Maybe I can get Arnold to come in early tomorrow so I can come with you to

Norman's funeral. The murderer isn't locked up yet. It might still be dangerous for you to be there alone."

"I wish I could go too," Ellie said, "but we told Mack's mother that we'd be on the ten o'clock ferry to the Vineyard for the week-end. You'd better not get in any trouble while I'm gone."

"I'll be fine. How much trouble can I get into with two policemen standing guard?"

Ellie gave her a stern look. "You forget that I know you."

CHAPTER 40

On Saturday morning Iris sat at her kitchen table, dressed in a navy linen dress appropriate for a summer funeral. There was still half an hour before she had to leave. She had finished scanning the Boston Globe—nothing much there. Her eyes lighted on the turkish-taffy pink boom box that Ellie had retrieved from Raven's room on their walk home the night before. Okay, now she *was* curious. What the hell was on this cassette? She popped it in.

Scratchy sounds, then... "I'm telling you, Adam, I'm making a recording of this." That sounded like Norman. "It's my life insurance policy."

"What the hell, Norman. I never agreed to this." Adam's voice.

Iris sat up straight at the sound of the familiar voices.

"You don't have a choice. I saw you push Carey over the handrail, so what's to keep you from killing me too? I'm putting this in a safe place in case anything happens to me."

"You agreed to keep quiet if I'd get you Carey's notebook. That's our deal. I'm sure you'll use it to make a fortune."

"By keeping quiet about what you did I'm risking being an accessory to murder. I don't even know what's in the damn notebook. Carey may have been drawing cartoons for all I know."

"Oh, it's not cartoons. You get 2 minutes to look through it... starting now!"

O... MY... GOD, Iris thought. I've got to call Detective Malone NOW!

"Okay. This is good stuff. I can work with this. Here's the money. You get ten thousand cash, and no more." That's all that Adam made off of this? "We have a stand-off now," Norman went on. "We both have a big interest in keeping this hushed up. So from now on, we have no more communication. The police are investigating Carey's death. I don't think anyone was paying any attention to who was where at the party. But if the police do figure out that you killed him, our deal is that you leave me out of it. I just followed the two of you to make one last try to get Carey to come work for me."

"All right, fine. You keep your mouth closed, and you make your fortune off of Carey's wacko ideas. You say anything to the cops, and I drag you down with me."

"You get my silence and ten grand in your pocket. Don't even think about hitting me up for more later."

"*Adios, amigo.*" Sound of chairs scraping and then... nothing.

Iris was dialing Detective Malone's cell phone number before the tape ended.

Damn. The answering machine message.

"Detective Malone, it's Iris Reid. You need to arrest Adam Lincoln immediately. I have a cassette tape that Norman made that got mixed in with some of his paperwork. I just played it and it's Norman saying that Adam killed our classmate twenty years ago. Adam must have killed him because Norman was going to expose him. I'm not sure exactly why he'd do that now, but you need to arrest Adam. He's supposed to be at the funeral this morning. Please call me on my cell phone."

She slipped the cassette into its envelope, then put that inside a ziploc bag, trying to minimize fingerprints like she'd seen on TV.

Did she have time to call Ellie to tell her what was on the tape? Consulting her watch, she grabbed her keys instead and headed out the door. She didn't want to be late for this funeral.

CHAPTER 41

S topped at a red light a block from the cemetery entrance, Iris fished in her purse for the map and instructions Claire had e-mailed her. Norman, unsurprisingly, had arranged to be buried in one of the oldest and most significant cemeteries in the United States. Mount Auburn Cemetery sat on 175 acres on the western edge of Cambridge, well known for its plantings, birds, and its interesting crypts as much as for its renowned inhabitants. How many people can be buried in a National Historic Landmark? Strangely enough, she knew of two. The last time she'd been here had been for Carey's funeral.

Norman had done his research so that he could be surrounded in perpetuity by Cabots and Lodges, not to mention Longfellow, Hawthorne, and Buckminster Fuller. Iris had a feeling that many of the attendees would be there to see, and be seen in, the magnificent setting more than to pay homage to Norman Meeker. In all her years passing it on her way to the nearby Shaw's Market, this was only the second time Iris had ever been inside the cemetery's imposing granite gates. But, this morning, she didn't have time to focus on its historic import. Her priority was to find Detective Malone quickly.

A little before ten, she pulled in through the north entrance and navigated up the hill toward Bigelow Chapel, following Claire's map. This place was Disney World for landscape architects, the grounds punctuated with topiaries, obelisks, statues and mausoleums resembling garden follies. The instructions said to park on any street without a green line down the middle, but this would not be easy. There was quite a crowd already assembled. She drove past the Chapel, a Gothic Revival mini-cathedral, and made a right-hand turn down Pine Avenue, finally spotting a space just big enough for the Jeep.

As she trotted back up the hill to Chapel Avenue, she saw a black BMW station wagon with New York plates. She clutched her purse, with the cassette tape inside it but something lured her over to peer into the car. Of course nothing incriminating was left out in plain sight. She bent down to study the rear tire. The tiny pieces of pea gravel stuck in the tread didn't prove anything because they had driven this car up Norman's driveway to the Friday night dinner.

"What are you doing? Get away from our car, Iris!" She heard that unmistakable voice.

"I'm thinking of getting one of these. Does it get good gas mileage?"

Alyssa made a disgusted "Tsk" as she opened the car door, grabbed a sweater, beeped the auto-lock, and stood there, hands on hips, waiting for Iris to leave.

Iris tried to look nonchalant as she headed up the hill toward the chapel. She was relieved to see Detective Malone and Connors huddled together by a conspicuously unmarked car and rushed over.

"Did you get my message on your cell? I've brought the cassette tape. You've got to listen to it." She produced the ziploc bag.

Detective Malone held it up and examined it through the plastic. He smiled wryly. "We will, and I have some questions about how it came into your possession. If you could come down to the station after the service, I'll take your statement."

Iris groaned. She was spending way too much time at that station for an innocent bystander. "Just be sure to arrest Adam before he gets away. He's the murderer."

"Yes, ma'am."

Was he being sarcastic? She shot a narrow-eyed look at his back. At least she'd gotten rid of the hot potato. Now she'd be out of danger. She caught sight of C.C. planted on a bench across from the chapel staring at a large granite sphinx. Iris hadn't had time to absorb the full impact of the cassette tape, but it had to mean that C.C. was off their suspect list. Iris walked over and sank down next to her. "So, you came. Wild place— huh?"

"I feel like a marker in a giant board game and I've been moved from the Egyptian Gate to the Towering

Linden Tree to the Gothic Chapel to the Sphinx." C.C. said just before a screech of bagpipe music assaulted their ears.

"And now you've rolled 'Back 1 space to the Gothic Chapel,'" Iris shouted. "It's show time!"

A nondescript man and two adolescent boys stood stiffly on the chapel steps. From their uncomfortable downcast expressions and general resemblance to Norman, the boys must be the sons, brought home from school by Barb after all. The man, dressed in a somber suit, wore a look of professional sympathy and propriety—probably charged by the funeral home with tending to Norman's only family. Iris couldn't believe that Barb hadn't come along, at least to give her sons moral support. All three wore white lilies in their lapels, and they looked rooted there as if stuck in a receiving line. Unsure of the etiquette, Iris shook the boys' hands and mumbled something sympathetic. C.C. followed suit.

The chapel consisted of a single nave, without side aisles or transept, leading up to a large, gaudily colored stained glass window in front. An awful thought occurred to Iris. Oh, God, this had better not be an open coffin. She couldn't face those leaden eyes again.

A large, heavily polished mahogany casket rested on a stand in the chancel, its lid, mercifully, closed. Iris and C.C. slid into a pew on the left—the bride's side. She twisted around and saw Detective Connors sitting in the back row with another man, telegraphing 'cop' despite their formal dark suits. G.B. sat half-way down the pews, his head bowed in a prayerful pose. She noticed Alyssa in the second row near Claire, but no sign of Adam. Detective Malone must have already taken him off to the station. Why hadn't Alyssa gone with him? Maybe she hadn't seen him taken away and assumed that Adam was still outside. Or maybe he hadn't come after all. The two dozen or so other mourners were probably from Meeker Enterprises, earning their overtime by fleshing out the crowd.

An unseen organist had been playing a dirge-like tune guaranteed to depress the audience, but now segued into something more lively. The Meeker boys and their minder progressed slowly down the aisle to the front pew, followed by an overdressed minister exuding a bit too much pomp for the circumstance. He turned grandly at a podium up front and let his purple robe settle. The eulogy, delivered in a loud plummy voice, with an overtone of breakfast sherry, was so flattering that Iris suspected Norman was its author. Her mind kept going back to the cassette tape. Would its text be admissible in court? She thought that she remembered from a TV show that one participant had to be present for the opposing lawyer to question. What happens if the witness is dead and leaves a tape behind? Let it go, Iris. It's not your problem to make the case. Now that the police had Adam, maybe they could match his DNA to something.

As the minister rumbled on, Iris considered Norman. Since she had heard his cold voice on the tape her estimation of him had changed from selfish jerk to heartless monster. How had she missed seeing that side of him? What kind of person witnesses a murder and doesn't report it because he sees the chance to get something he wants out of it? Isn't that kind of behavior considered psychopathic? Or is it sociopathic? She could never remember the difference from Psych 101. What a pair Norman and Adam were! And poor Carey...

After a closing song—its words helpfully printed in the program—six men from the front row stood up and surrounded the coffin. Resting the support poles on their shoulders, they slowly filed out, followed by the boys, heads down. The rows of attending mourners followed, front row to back, peeling out of the pews right and left into a smooth flow to the door. Alyssa glared at Iris as she passed, no doubt wondering why she and C.C. were sitting together. The temporary congregation spilled out into the road, dividing around a black FDR-era hearse, complete with running boards, that was being loaded with Norman's remains. Everyone scrambled to their own cars to join the long line forming behind the hearse.

The cemetery roads wound up and down in a serpentine, passing mausoleums resembling mini-temples. Some plots had their turf defined by wrought-iron fences. The rolling procession wended its way toward the rear of the property where, for a price, one could purchase prime real estate overlooking Willow Pond.

Iris had to hand it to Norman. This was a beautiful spot. Too bad it was paid for by Carey's life. She couldn't help contrasting this pompous ceremony with Carey's simple one, Norman's prime plot with Carey's unadorned gravestone in a crowded field. She waited in her car for the ushers to carry the casket over to a contraption ready to lower it into the grave. Most of the

Norman Meeker Enterprises staff, once reunited with their cars, had taken the opportunity to escape. So it was a smaller group that she now joined, clustered by the fresh grave site near Willow Pond path. Iris noticed that Alyssa had drifted away from the group. The minister said a final prayer, arms uplifted dramatically. The two boys awkwardly threw clumps of dirt on top of the casket, making thudding sounds with a dull ring of finality. Iris felt woozy from the strong smell of newly cut grass, or maybe it was the momentarily pathetic tableau of the fatherless boys. They, at least, were innocent.

As the ceremony wound down, C.C. approached, saying "I'm going in to the station now with the Detective to give him a statement about that leverage business."

Iris looked over to see Detective Connors watching them. She nodded. "Good. I'm going to go visit another grave."

CHAPTER 42

Malone turned to the department's audio-visual guy, "Does the office even have a cassette player anymore?"

"Of course we do." He seemed affronted. "We have everything in this new set-up." The AV technician snapped the tape into the player and the miniature spools began to rotate.

After a few seconds of scratchy static, the words came through clearly: "I'm telling you, Adam, that I'm making a recording of this. It's my life insurance policy."

"What the hell, Norman. I never agreed to this."

"You don't have a choice. I saw you push Carey over the handrail, so what's to keep you from killing me too? I'm putting this in a safe place in case anything happens to me."

The detective's mouth had transformed from a line to a circle. "Stop the tape! Hang on." He pressed the speed dial on his cell.

"Did you find Adam Lincoln yet?"

"No. His wife said he felt sick and went back to the hotel. He took their car. She left from the chapel with the professor. I'm headed back now with the magazine lady. She's going to make a statement about that phone call that Reynolds made last week."

"Listen, Connors. Lincoln is our guy. We've got some proof on this tape. Is it the same hotel they were in before? Go pick him up. Put the magazine lady in a cab. I'll send back-up, so wait for it. He might be packing."

"Roger that. I'll call when I've got him."

Malone turned back to the AV guy. "Okay. Play me the rest."

***

"He's not in his room. The car's not here. The receptionist said that she hasn't seen him. Whadda you want me to do?"

"Damn— he must have figured we're onto him. Pick up the wife and bring her in. We've got to grab him before he can disappear." Malone slammed down his desk phone.

C.C. regarded Detective Malone sullenly from under the bangs of her pageboy.

His furious gray eyes glared back at her. "Lemme get this straight. You're saying Will Reynolds told you he intended to blackmail Norman Meeker into backing him in some development deal? In other words our first victim was going to try to get money from our second victim, but you didn't think this was worth mentioning to the police? Anything else that you haven't bothered to tell us about?"

"Well, since Will never got there, I thought it didn't matter. And he didn't say 'blackmail'. I would've remembered that. I'm coming here voluntarily to make sure you have all the facts, even the ones that seem unimportant. Will was my friend."

Malone kneaded his right temple, eyes closed. A knock on his door brought his head back up.

The young plainclothes detective from the funeral leaned his head into the room. "They all left, Detective Malone. I checked them off the list like you said."

Malone walked out to the hall and closed the door behind him. "Adam Lincoln looks like our guy and he's still on the loose. So, no one's left at the cemetery, right?"

"Well, the Reid woman was still there when I left. I think she was making a phone call, but she wasn't on my list."

C.C. opened the door and volunteered "Iris said she was going to walk around the cemetery for awhile."

"Oh, shit. DiAngelo, get back there and find her NOW before we have another body on our hands. And YOU," he turned to C.C., "sit down while I decide whether to book you for withholding evidence!"

CHAPTER 43

Maybe now she could reach Ellie. She wandered down to her car and retrieved her cell phone. Ellie's voice mail message came on. She was probably on the ferry to the Vineyard.

"Ellie, it's me. Call my cell ASAP! I have news."

She rested her head back against the driver's seat and let the events of the morning settle in her mind. Norman had been a terrible person. She couldn't get over how she had underestimated his greed. She and Ellie had been right about Carey's death being a murder. Adam had killed him and he must have killed Will and Norman too, alibi or no alibi. Was he insane?

She wanted to call Luc. She wanted to hear his completely sane, reassuring voice. The clock on her dashboard read 11:21. He'd be catching up on sleep, so she wouldn't wake him.

Carey's memorial service had been in this general area of the cemetery. Wasn't it in a field just beyond that ridge in the direction of the Crematorium? She'd recognize the spot when she saw it. As she realized that she'd finally be able to tell her friend that his murderer had been unmasked, the space between her shoulders relaxed.

The trees shimmered with light. The green of the manicured grass almost hurt her eyes. She wandered up the hill to examine a modern sculpture—a tall, twisting bronze plane that suggested redemption and release. She found this modern expression of an afterlife far more moving than the clunky angels and saints standing solemn guard nearby. The soaring bronze was encircled by feathery plants that, Iris suspected, would give her hay fever if she lingered, so she kept moving. Her eye was caught by a prominent headstone. It listed three people with three birth dates and two dates of deaths. She wondered how the third person, born in 1927, felt about some impatient stonecutter itching to finish his commission. Also, wasn't it tacky to lump people together on one headstone? 'Thrift above all' was the Yankee motto, she mused.

Her own parents had been cremated, according to their wishes. She and her brother had scattered their ashes from the top of a mountain near their childhood home in Norwich, Vermont. Would it have been more comforting for her to have had a grave site to visit? Probably not. She still felt her mother's presense. Sometimes she would carry on whole conversations with her mother, taking both sides, as Sheba watched her warily.

Iris wandered on, stopping to read handy tree identification tags. Her horticultural knowledge, outside of flowers, was thin. She was passing a particularly ugly modern mausoleum when she heard a sound, footsteps crunching quietly on the stone path behind her. Was someone following her? She ducked quickly behind the tiny building and ran around to peek from the other side in time to see a man's leg disappear.

Where was everyone? The public all seemed to be occupied elsewhere on this warm June Saturday. Even the teams of green-uniformed gardeners, walkie-talkies clipped to their belts, must have been tending the grounds in other sections of the vast cemetery. Her cell phone was back in the Jeep. She needed to make her way back to a more populated area.

She was overreacting. It was probably an innocent mourner laying flowers at a loved one's grave. She rounded the next corner and saw his back. With icy calm, her brain registered: Adam.

He must have hidden during the funeral. She tried to silently back away but a twig snapped underfoot. He rounded on her and she rocketed up a hill, dodging headstones. Please, God, don't let me twist an ankle. Her eyes raked the landscape for a hiding place. Maybe I can make it to that clump of trees. Can he see me? She zigzagged behind mausoleums and bushes but then tripped on a sprinkler head sticking up in the grass and sprawled forward, skinning her palms as she went down. She could hear him wheezing in the distance behind her and scrambled back to her feet. She didn't stop to look. Her sides burned and she gasped for breath. A huge Weeping Willow appeared on the hilltop and she willed herself towards it. She could try to hide inside its trailing boughs, inside its cave of space, but knew it wouldn't take long for Adam to guess where she was.

She pushed through the silvery branches and bent down from the waist to breathe deeply. Focus, Iris! You have to defend yourself. What good was her brown belt if she was out of practice? At least her school of karate, Uechiryu, emphasized close-in fighting. That was all she'd have room for. Time to test her skills.

She slumped into Sanchin defensive position, elbows protecting ribs, palms up, thumbs tucked in, and waited, practicing long, deep breathing. In less than a minute Adam breached the boughs, charging toward her like a spooked horse, shuddering with rage. He lunged out at her, grabbing for her wrists.

"Where did you find that tape? You gave it to the cops, you bitch! Why didn't you stay out of this?" he howled.

She slashed down on his forearms, knocking his hands apart and attempted to side-kick him in the knee. "Are you going to kill me too, like you killed Will and Norman?"

Damn—too slow. He grabbed her foot, pulling her down onto her back.

"Norman killed Will. He was gonna kill me too," he growled, his shoulders heaving. He lifted his foot to stomp on her face. She rolled aside and sprang back up. She faked a left-foot kick, followed by an actual right-foot snap kick to the groin. Then spinning around, gathering momentum, she rammed her braced left elbow into his ribs, and drove her right palm upwards into his chin. A sharp crunch come from his jaw. He doubled over and crumpled to the ground.

"It's over, Adam. Malone knows you killed Carey," she spat out, trying to shake away the explosion of pain in her skinned palm.

He clamped a hand onto her leg and said through gritted teeth, "Then it won't matter if I kill *you*."

She tried to sweep her leg free but his arms were like tentacles. He managed to pull himself up to a standing position, then clamp his hands around her throat. She couldn't break his grip. He started squeezing. Purple streaks appeared across her blurred vision and she felt herself start to sway. With the energy she had left, she latched onto his right wrist with both hands and, using gravity and her own body weight, she dropped down, taking his right arm with her. Then gulping in air, she shot up from a crouch, shoving his arm up his back as hard as she could. She kept pushing until she heard a satisfying pop, followed by his collapse on the ground.

She leaned over, hands on knees, trying to see straight. She tasted blood, her throat and hand throbbed, but she needed to escape while she could. Pushing through the branches, she ran out into an open field, searching for help. She made a quick decision to follow the winding road back towards the front gate. Painfully, she began to trot, her lungs burning. Cresting a hill, she thought she saw a car heading her way. She raised her arms and tried to shout to get the driver's attention but her voice came out strangled. Like a mirage, a police cruiser floated towards her, picking up speed as it got closer. She sobbed with relief. Sergeant DiAngelo spoke into his radio, "I've found the Reid woman. Send a bus."

CHAPTER 44

Two days later, on a sultry Monday afternoon, Iris adjusted the telephoto lens as she peered through the viewfinder at Norman's house. It sat nestled in the hill, its windows looking blank and undisturbed. Shafts of sunlight broke through the trees. Sheba lay dozing on the grass nearby, snoring softly.

Luc, from behind her, lifted her hair and gently kissed the bruises on her neck. "I could kill that asshole."

"It's not easy. I tried... Hey, you're distracting the photographer."

"How does the rest of you feel?" He kept kissing.

"Bruised, pummeled, and scraped. The hospital docs say no internal injuries. When they sprung me this morning, they said I just needed time to mend. Adam didn't make out so well. I managed to dislocate his shoulder and crack his jaw."

"Ouch, I hope he's in agony." Luc eased down onto the grass, propping himself on his elbows. "But remind me to watch my step around you. How did you learn how to fight like that?"

"I've taken some karate. He's strong though. I almost blacked out when he was trying to choke me."

"I'm not sure I can listen to that part without becoming murderous myself." He yanked up some grass. "Okay, you've promised to fill me in on all the details. You have my total attention."

"I like having your total attention," she smirked down at him, then squeezed the shutter.

"You have it a lot, you know." He regarded her through half-closed eyes. "So, it's all over? Adam was behind everything? What happened to his unshakable alibi for Friday afternoon."

"That's just it," she said. "*Norman* killed Will. Detective Malone was explaining things to me while I waited in the hospital for all those damned tests. He was able to get quite a bit out of Adam before Alyssa charged in with her lawyer."

"Wait a minute. Maybe you should start at the beginning with Carey."

"Okay. Adam *did* kill Carey twenty years ago. Adam had been apoplectic about the drubbing he'd gotten at his final review from the same critics who'd idolized Carey, so Adam set out to humiliate him at the party. But after he'd gotten Carey stoned and out on the balcony, Adam couldn't resist giving him a push. Norman had followed them as far as the bedroom and witnessed the whole thing, so Adam swore he'd get him Carey's notebook of inventions in return for his silence." Iris unscrewed the long lens from the camera, then the camera from the tripod, and headed to a new vantage point ten feet away.

Luc hopped up and followed, then flopped back down onto the grass. "An ethical guy, our Norman."

"No dummy either," she said, affixing a wide-angle lens. "He later recorded Adam discussing this arrangement with him, and said the tape would be sent to the authorities if he, Norman, ever met with an untimely death."

"This was on that cassette you found in his papers about the house project?"

"Right. He'd probably been listening to it in his office before his Sunday meeting with Adam and had forgotten to put it back in the safe." Iris tipped her head as she studied the shot. "Norman kept it in an envelope with 'Linc' written on the outside, so Claire assumed it was Lincoln renovation paperwork. 'Linc' really meant Adam's nickname."

"Telling what he'd seen to the police back when it happened would have been a lot safer than making this recording. He was the only witness to a murder."

"True, but then Norman wouldn't have gotten the notebook. He'd already tried to hire Carey. He knew how valuable those ideas were."

"This is like a chess game. They were holding each other in check but neither of them could checkmate the other."

"That's exactly right, and the stalemate held for all those years after Carey's death. Then Norman upset the balance by holding the reunion party at his fancy new house. He was trying to get C.C. to publish it in her magazine so he could pimp his profile on the social scene, but he ended up rubbing Adam's nose in how well he had done on the strength of Carey's notebook." She bracketed the shot with three quick exposures.

"How did Will fit into the picture?"

"After C.C. finally revealed that Will was planning to hit up Norman for money, using his knowledge of how Norman had built his company as leverage, the police think Norman responded by suggesting a meeting on Friday to go over the business proposition. Instead, he tasered Will in the car, drove over to Fresh Pond, injected him with that syringe of poison, then rolled his body down from the parking lot into the woods. He must have figured he'd frame me for Will's murder by dumping the body where he knew I walked my dog every afternoon." Her teeth locked over her lower lip.

"Why? What did he have against you?"

"I don't think I was supposed to take it personally. He just needed a fall guy and I was convenient. He knew my habits. I guess that's why he left me his Porsche—as a sort of 'no hard feelings' gift, a reward to enjoy if I was clever enough to wriggle out of the frame he was creating."

"Wow—a shrink would have a field day with this guy. So that explains Carey and Will, but what about Norman's death? I assume that Adam did that. But why?"

"That's actually the most logical of the three murders. Adam admitted that he set up a meeting with

Norman for Sunday afternoon. Norman must have figured that Adam wanted to shake him down for more money. He might have even killed Will partially to warn Adam off. But basically, Norman was in clean-up mode to get rid of anyone who knew about the source of his wealth. He was in his kitchen ready for Adam, with his stun gun and another loaded syringe. I'll bet he arranged to have me there at the house so I could be framed for Adam's murder as well as Will's."

She removed the wide-angle lens and went on, "I guess he hoped to surprise Adam, like he had with Will, but Adam overpowered him, grabbed the needle, and shot him up with it—he was hoisted with his own petard. Then Adam heard me drive up, so he dragged Norman's body downstairs, stashed it in the wine refrigerator to confuse the time of death, then drove off from the garage, figuring that no one would find Norman for another day. It makes my flesh crawl to think that I might have run into Adam if I had arrived earlier."

He threw her a worried look and she reminded herself to soft-pedal the truly scary parts of her story.

"Where did Norman get this drug that he put in the syringes?"

"The police think he was able to synthesize it himself in his lab. They found one of the components of this drug in a refrigerator there. It would have been almost impossible to detect if the police hadn't found that first syringe with some traces of the drug still in it."

"What I don't get is why Adam, as Norman's murderer, would come back for the guy's funeral?" Luc asked.

"There you have me. The police are guessing that he might have been planning to search for the cassette tape. Or maybe he wanted to find out if the police suspected him. Alyssa, of course, is claiming that she had no idea about anything that Adam had been up to."

"Do you buy that?"

"From Lady Macbeth? Doubtful. But unless he turns on her, it'll be impossible to prove. I still can't get my head around the fact that Norman killed Will and tried to kill Adam. He seemed to be such a wimp. I guess, with his inflated opinion of himself, he considered these killings to be justified. I worked for the guy for a year. I'm glad I didn't do anything to piss him off." She clicked on a short telephoto lens, set the tripod lower, and tilted the camera up at the house.

"I'd never thought of architecture as such a dangerous profession."

"Our class was an unusually poisonous group. Most of them were just snarky and backstabbing. But then there was Carey's death and I was convinced that one of them was actually a murderer—but I didn't know which one. It turned out that *two* of them were murderers."

"I'll never look at architects the same way. Is the DA going to be able to prove the case against Adam? It seems like a lot of circumstantial evidence."

"He'll definitely spend time behind bars for Carey's murder and his attack on me. They even tracked the envelope bomb to him. Norman's tape was iffy as evidence, but that became moot when Detective Malone played it in the interview room and Adam started babbling out a confession before his lawyer could muzzle him."

"I like it when a sleaze bag like Adam hands the DA a confession. Just like on TV," he looked amused, propped up on one elbow.

"Yeah, Adam isn't the sharpest knife in the drawer. Whether there's a clear case to convict him of killing Norman is another matter. But, you know, I don't care as much. Those two deserved each other. Now, Norman's dead, Adam will be locked up for a long time, and poor Carey will get some justice."

"Thanks to you, Sherlock. You ended up putting the pieces together."

"Detective Malone did admit that they couldn't figure out a motive for these killings until I pointed out their connection to Carey's murder and the cover-up. You know what's ironic about this whole thing?"

"No, what?" He smoothed the hair back from her face.

"I never would have been suspicious in the first place if the autopsy hadn't turned up drugs in Carey's system. I knew that he'd never intentionally take them. But if I'd known that his drugging had been a spiteful joke, I would never have been convinced that he'd been murdered and that I had to try to find his killer. I doubt that I would have gone to the reunion."

"Hmmm. So Adam's headed to jail for killing Carey because he didn't tell you that he pulled a prank on your friend."

"Yeah—ironic." Minutes passed in silence. Iris gazed up again at the modern structure of wood and glass. "I've got all the shots I need." she said, packing up her equipment into her camera bag. C.C.'s crew would be there the next week to collect their own images of it for the pages of *cuttingedgedecor*. Luc replanted the realtor's 'For Sale' sign back by the driveway. Damn, this was one of her favorite creations.

CHAPTER 45

Four months later, Iris gazed out of the office she now shared with Ellie at Harvard's Graduate School of Design. The slate on the High Victorian spire of Memorial Hall was a riot of colors against the approaching gloom of an October afternoon. Stacks of hand-outs, an empty can of Diet Coke, and her macbook air lay scattered across her desk.

"I can't believe we're the ones giving the critiques now. It still feels bizarre." Ellie said from her adjacent desk.

Iris swiveled toward her co-professor. "If we can't strong-arm some Very Important Architects to be guest critics, we'll never be able to parlay this into a full-time gig. I hear Alyssa's getting Richard Meier to fly up."

Ellie groaned and Sheba, lying at Iris' feet, looked up with concern.

At that moment, Iris' cell phone twanged the guitar intro to *'Stand by Your Man'*.

"Luc changed my ringtone," Iris explained, then startled at the words 'Meeker Enterprises' on the caller i.d.

Ellie whispered "Who?" and Iris wrote out Meeker Ent. on a scrap of paper and rotated it for her to see.

As she recognized Barb's voice, Iris sank back into her chair and mouthed "Barb" at Ellie.

Ellie slid her chair closer to Iris' desk to eavesdrop. They had both read in the previous week's *Globe* about Barb taking over Norman's company. A photo had shown her in a sleek suit, her hair newly styled, looking every inch the confident CEO.

"Yes, I read about it. Congratulations," As Iris listened, a smile played across her face. "You say it'll be in the paper soon? Fantastic. That means a lot. Thanks for telling me, Barb. Bye, now."

"So? Tell me!"

"She's changing the name of the Meeker geo-thermal energy system to the Sorensen Geo-thermal energy system to honor Carey, 'its actual inventor.'"

Ellie nodded her head solemnly, fixing serious eyes on Iris'. Iris nodded back with eyebrows raised. This act didn't change anything that had happened, but it shifted Iris' world one significant notch on its axis, and everything else would need to adjust.

"Come on. Let's go toast Carey," Ellie said. They grabbed their coats and locked the office behind them.

Out in the hall floated the laughter and excited talk of students caught up for the first time in a world of intense competition and limitless dreams.

About the Author

Like her sleuth, Susan Cory practices residential architecture from a turreted office. Like Iris, she has a brown belt in Karate. She even went to her own twentieth Harvard Graduate School of Design reunion, but no one was murdered. She lives in Cambridge, Ma. with her architect husband, Dan, and her bossy mutt, not a basset hound.

Made in the USA
Lexington, KY
03 December 2012